SEASII

JE.

&

MADDY MADDSON

JENNA ST. JAMES BOOKS

Ryli Sinclair Mystery Series Order
Picture Perfect Murder
Girls' Night Out Murder
Old-Fashioned Murder
Bed, Breakfast, and Murder
Veiled in Murder
Bachelorettes and Bodies
Rings, Veils, and Murder
Last Stop Murder
Gold, Frankincense, and a Merry Murder

Sullivan Sisters Mystery Series Order
Murder on the Vine
Burning Hot Murder
PrePEAR to Die
Tea Leaves, Jealousy, and Murder

Copper Cove Mystery Series
Seaside & Homicide

A Witch in Time Series (Shared World)
Time After Time (Book 3)

DEDICATION

Special thanks to my step-daughter, Maddy, for suggesting we write a co-authored series together. Not only are you a great BETA reader, but you're also an amazingly talented writer.

Thank you Jessica King and Janice Booth...I'm so glad I finally got to include you guys in a book series!

Special thanks also to Point Arena, CA...for giving my fictitious town a real-life base from which to launch.

Chapter 1

"We're still on for tonight, right?" Peyton Patterson, my best friend since kindergarten, grinned hopefully at me. "We're still going?"

I sighed and shifted my backpack on my shoulder as we continued walking down the street. Thirteen years of public education had taught me that the downfall of being studious was always having a sore back and shoulder muscles. "I guess. Not much else to do in the big town of Copper Cove on a Friday night, is there?"

"Brynn O'Connell," Peyton said, "stop being a fun sucker!"

She bumped her hip against mine, and I teetered precariously from the sudden jostling. For some reason, I had a hard time staying upright most days. You wouldn't think I'd be clumsy from the looks of me...sturdy, average height and build, with a compact torso most athletes yearned for. And yet, for reasons unbeknownst to me, it didn't help me maintain my center of gravity.

"Copper Cove can be plenty exciting," Peyton insisted.

I rolled my eyes.

Our sleepy seaside town of about nine thousand sat along the natural cove of the Pacific Ocean in Mendocino County. Like a lot of coastal towns, the houses and storefronts were bright and cheerful. And while I loved being able to look out my bedroom window and watch the boats and whales go by, I wished there was more to do. Nothing exciting ever happened in this town...no matter what Peyton said.

"Think there'll be any cute boys there tonight?" Peyton asked.

Most kids our age didn't know how to take Peyton. She could be intimidating at first glance. She stood nearly six feet tall, had long blonde hair she always wore in a haphazard bun on top of her head, and was naturally beautiful and slim. She was the type of girl boys ogled from afar because they were too scared to approach her and other girls envied—hence she was often bullied by our peers. Add in the fact that she was in line to be our class valedictorian and was an all-around genius...most kids found it was just easier to make fun of her than befriend and get to know her.

Especially boys.

I didn't have boy problems, and I didn't want them. I learned at an early age boys were nothing but trouble. My mom dropped me off on my Grams' doorstep the minute I was born and took off with the guy who got her pregnant. He'd said he wasn't *ready* for a baby. And seventeen years later, I guess he still wasn't.

I occasionally hear from my mom, but not often. Which is fine by me. Like Grams said, she chose her life.

"What're you gonna wear?" Peyton asked. "I'm thinking about wearing my—"

She was cut off by a loud horn. We both stopped along the sidewalk and watched with apprehension as two of our classmates stood up in Seth Graham's convertible and jeered at us.

"Nerd!"

"Freak!"

They peeled away, screaming with laughter.

"Ya know," I said dryly, "just once *I'd* like to be the nerd and *you* be the freak."

Peyton forced a laugh as we continued down the street. "Maybe this time you *were* the nerd," Peyton joked. "You never know!"

Yes, I did. I was bullied for another reason. I was a freak. I was the abandoned girl no one wanted...well, except for a Grams most people pegged as a witch who sold potions and spells out of her witchy store.

A complete lie.

Grams owned Winnie's Apothecary, located on the main strip in town. A self-proclaimed herbalist, she dealt in homeopathic remedies. And while I loved my Grams to pieces, her job had put a target on my back since my first day of school. Like I really needed the extra help. Having kids poke fun at you because your mom didn't want you and your grandma was a witch sucked. Big time. But I tried not to dwell on it. I considered myself blessed to have a friendship like I had with Peyton.

"Don't listen to them," Peyton said. "Seth's just jealous. *His* mom had to go to school for years to become a botanist and have people respect her, while your Grams is renowned for her remedies."

I gave her a get-real look.

"*And*," Peyton continued, "*his* mom just identifies plants, while your Grams gets to use them to heal people."

There was a lot more to being a botanist than just identifying plants, but I appreciated what Peyton was trying to do. Shifting my backpack to my other shoulder, I slipped my arm through hers. "You're the *best* best friend a girl could ever have."

Peyton grinned down at me. "I know. I take my job seriously."

We rounded the corner and hit Main Street. It ran the full length of town along the coastline and was jam-packed with buildings. Copper Cove hustled and bustled with tourists from April to September. The seasonal holidays brought in people, but nothing like the spring and summer months.

Which is another reason why Peyton was so intent on going to the Copper Cove Fall Festival tonight. The last time we had a town social was back in September when we did a back-to-school/end-of-summer shindig. This weekend's October Fall Festival would end tomorrow night, and the town wouldn't do another gathering until the Christmas Bizarre in December.

I gasped and yanked Peyton to a stop when I saw Mayor Barrow and Prudence Livingston in a heated debate outside City Hall. The mere sight of Prudence Livingston usually had me shaking in anger and fear. At least once a week for as long as I could remember, she would stand in front of Grams' store passing out flyers and telling anyone who'd listen that my Grams was a witch who did the devil's work. Grams just laughed her off, but Prudence Livingston was what my nightmares were made of.

"We can cross the street and go to your Grams' shop that way," Peyton said. "We don't need to stop by Sisters Bakery today."

I pushed down the fear that bubbled up inside me. "No, it's fine. Besides, it's nice to see her making trouble for someone else besides Grams."

Peyton reached down and took my hand as we slowly made our way toward Mayor Barrow and Prudence. By now their voices were raised enough I could hear what they were saying. I was pretty shocked they'd openly make a spectacle of themselves in public like they were.

"I mean it, Pru," Mayor Barrow snapped. "You even *think* to make trouble for me and the town on this new land development plan, and I'll bury you so deep in the sand they'll *never* find your body."

My eyes grew wide at his threat, but I kept my head down as Peyton and I attempted to shuffle past without bringing attention to ourselves.

"That plan is bad business for this town. *My* town," Prudence snarled. "I'll make whatever trouble I have to to make sure this deal doesn't happen. The only people it'll benefit are you and the developers. Lining your own pockets while your citizens suffer. Shame on you, Louis Barrow!"

"Keep your mouth shut," Mayor Barrow threatened. "Or you won't be able to open it and make trouble for anyone else."

Oomph!

I picked up my head as I bounced off the body in front of me.

"Sorry, kid," Peter Anders said absently as he thrust me aside. "Mayor Barrow! Prudence Livingston! Great to see you two out and about."

"Anders!" Mayor Barrow said jovially as he stuck his hand out. "Always good to see you."

"Let's go," Peyton hissed.

I latched on to my backpack, and we all but sprinted down the street toward Sisters Bakery and Coffee Shop. Twin sisters, Janice and Jessica, owned the store together. Janice made the pastries and Jessica served up specialty coffees and teas. Peyton and I stopped by every day after school to load up on caffeine and post pics of our goodies on Instagram.

Peyton pushed open the door, and I immediately went to my happy place. Nothing brought me greater joy than a large mocha with whipped cream and a chocolate croissant. Being a creature of habit, Janice always made sure to have at least one of the pastries set aside for me after school.

"What do you think that was about?" Peyton asked as we sat down at a table in front of the window overlooking Main Street. Grams' apothecary was catty-corner from where I sat.

"I have no idea," I said. "I'm just glad Prudence wasn't in her normal spot outside Grams' place. Woman gives me the creeps."

"And what was up with that Realtor guy just pushing you aside?" Peyton continued. "Brushing you off like lint on his jacket."

I shrugged. "Adults. Who can understand them?"

We snickered and continued to sip our caffeine miracles.

"Did you ever find out who trespassed on your property the other night and stole some of your Grams' garden stakes?" Peyton asked.

9

I shook my head. "No. It's the weirdest thing."

Two days ago, when Grams went to check on her potted plants, she discovered a couple of her twelve-inch garden stakes were missing. She'd had them made special. Gold, with a three by five frame at the top where Grams could write in the plant's name, and on the back on the gold nameplates were her initials. Why someone would want them was beyond me.

"Probably just kids playing a prank," Peyton said.

I shrugged. "We'll probably never see them again. Officer Casen came out and took down Grams' statement because she filed an official police report. He didn't offer much hope."

Tossing the empty cups in the trash can, Peyton and I waved goodbye to the sisters and walked back outside. I shifted my backpack again and was about to cross the street to the apothecary when Grams' front door opened and out walked the new girl in town, Raven Masters.

You couldn't miss her. She had alabaster skin, bright blue eyes, and the deep purple lipstick she always wore matched the dark purple hue of her hair dye. And black was pretty much her staple wardrobe color.

"Wonder what she bought?" Peyton mused.

"Probably eye of newt to put in one of her spells," I said.

Peyton chortled and we crossed the street. "Your grandma doesn't sell eye of newt." When I didn't say anything, Peyton's eyes grew huge. "Does she?"

I rolled my eyes. "Of course not!"

At least I didn't think so.

CHAPTER 2

"I put the dosage on there for you," Grams said to Bernice Trader as Peyton and I walked through the door of the apothecary.

"Oh, thank you, Winnie," Bernice said to Grams. "These hot flashes are killing me!"

Grams patted her on the arm. "It'll get better. Now, come on back and see me if you want that other remedy I told ya about." Grams winked conspiratorially at Bernice. "I promise it'll work like a charm."

Bernice's face turned pink. "I'll think about it, Winnie. Right now this is fine."

Grams nodded. "I understand. Let me ring this up for you."

Grams hurried over to the cash register to finalize Bernice's purchase as I set my backpack behind the counter. Bernice wandered over to the soaps and beauty products I'd recently started making for the store.

"These are lovely," Bernice said as she picked up soap after soap and sniffed.

"Thanks," I said.

The recently added beauty section was a bit of a fight between Grams and me. When I graduated in May, I wanted to go to college and earn a degree in pharmaceuticals and cosmetic science. My goal was to make high-end cosmetics for companies like Clinique, Estee Lauder, and YSL. It'd been my dream for as long as I could remember. Grams wanted me to follow in her footsteps and stay in Copper Cove to make my own line of natural cosmetics and homemade bath products for the apothecary. We were constantly at odds over my future plans.

But, I was a teenager, always hungry, and in constant need of money...so I shoved my principles aside when Grams said if I made natural remedies and beauty products she'd sell them in the apothecary for an eighty-twenty split in my favor. I couldn't pass that deal up. A part of me knew she did it as a way to try and keep me connected to the shop and close by at the end of the school year. But my mind was made up. I'd already applied and been accepted to three different colleges. The closest was three hours away.

When Grams found out, she cried. I felt horrible, but I had big plans for my life, and they didn't include staying in Copper Cove forever. I guess deep down, I was a runner like my mom...even though I'd deck anyone who'd dare say that to my face.

"This one's my favorite," Peyton said as she handed a lavender and lemongrass soap to Bernice.

"Oh, it *is* lovely," Bernice agreed. "Hold up there, Winnie. Can you add this to my purchase, please?"

Peyton turned and winked at me.

"Thank you," I said.

Meow! Meow!

"I see you!" I picked up Jinx, our older-than-dirt black cat, and nuzzled his neck and listened to his rhythmic *purrrr*.

Jinx mystified me. Grams claimed he showed up on her doorstep the day my mom abandoned me...or in Grams' words the day my mom for once thought of someone else

12

other than herself and did an unselfish act. But no matter how you said it…it still hurt.

So that puts Jinx over the age of an average cat…seeing as how I'm going to be eighteen in March. I know it's probably not Guinness Book of World Records old, but still old nonetheless. I'd gone so far as to accuse Grams of switching out the cats once because I couldn't image how Jinx could still be so spry. But the truth was, I'd know.

And not just because I'd accidentally marked Jinx.

Once when I was eight I got it in my head I wanted to be a veterinarian. I shaved off a tiny spot on the top of Jinx's paw where I put in a pretend IV. Unfortunately, the hair never grew back, and to this day he had a bald patch there.

I know that really doesn't prove anything, and Grams could have still switched the cats out when I was younger. But I don't think so. I don't know how to explain it other than to say I have literally grown up my whole life with the same, protective black cat. Grams says I should just accept that sometimes magical things happen, but I personally think Jinx has some sort of chromosome or gene explanation for why he's so old.

The bell over the front door chimed as Bernice exited, and I waved Grams over.

"How was school?" she asked. "What's one thing you learn today?"

"That the mystery meat in the cafeteria is still a mystery," I quipped.

Grams and Peyton both laughed.

"You can be such a smarty pants sometimes," Grams chided me.

I shrugged. It was true. My mouth had gotten me more detentions than I cared to admit.

"Why was the new girl in here?" I asked.

Grams furrowed her brow. "What new girl? Oh, you mean that lovely girl Raven? Isn't she a breath of fresh air?"

Peyton and I goggled at Grams like she'd grown another head. A breath of fresh air? More like Wednesday Addams and Morticia got together and cloned a baby.

"Yeah," I said sarcastically. "What did that lovely breath of fresh air want in here?"

Grams tsked. "You know I don't gossip about what my customers buy. But let's just say she's very knowledgeable, and I hope she comes around a lot more." Grams reached over and cooed at Jinx. "I told her to stop by anytime. I enjoyed talking with her. In fact, she suggested you add some sage to your lavender and eucalyptus soap. And I couldn't agree more. Sage *is* a natural soother, you know?"

"I'm aware," I gritted.

I don't know why it upset me to have Raven come in here and criticize my soaps. It's not like I actually put my heart and soul into it. I made them for research purposes and a profit. But it still irked me that she suggested sage. Mainly because it was a good idea.

"Did you know she has a podcast where she talks about herbal and holistic living?" Grams asked.

"Nope," I said. "Sure didn't."

"She wants to interview me sometime," Grams said excitedly.

"You know about podcasts?" I asked.

14

Grams scoffed. "I'm not *that* old. Of course I know about podcasts." She turned to Peyton. "Are you having dinner with us tonight?"

Peyton shook her head. "Not tonight, Granny Winnie. I need to go home, change, and do a little primping for the festivities."

"Glad you girls have decided to go." Grams looked at me. "Raven said she'd be there. Maybe you two girls can open yourselves up to new experiences and friends."

"Subtle." I set Jinx down on the floor and picked up my backpack. "See you at home. Love ya, Grams."

Peyton and I headed out the door, Jinx on our heels. Usually, when I was alone, I'd take an immediate right and traverse the back way home down Ocean Drive. But since Peyton was with me, and she lived the next block up on Seaside, we made a left outside the apothecary.

Ocean Drive wound down to the right and then flattened out into a half-mile long road that dead ended at the Copper Cove Pier. Our house was situated between the streets of Ocean Drive and Seaside Drive on a ridge that extended out the side of the cliff. The backyard—or rather Grams' magical garden—faced the Pacific Ocean while the front door faced Seaside Drive. We spent eighty percent of our time either outside in the garden and outdoor kitchen area or the rooftop on the widow's walk.

Personally, I loved our widow's walk. It gave me an even higher vantage point to see out over Copper Cove. However, it was one of the feuding points with Milly Anders who owned the Seaside Bed and Breakfast directly across the street. She'd bought the bed and breakfast five years ago, and two years later she sued Grams over some ridiculous thing about how our widow's walk hindered her guests' view of the ocean.

Whatever. It wasn't like we'd recently built it there to hinder her view. It was built with the house over a hundred years ago. The judge dismissed her case, and the widow's walk stayed.

We hit the corner of Main and Seaside and Peyton pushed the crosswalk button.

"Meet up under the live oak at seven?" she asked.

"I'll be there," I promised.

She crossed over, and I made a left down Seaside. This section of town was sparse because Ocean Drive led straight to the Copper Cove Pier and ocean, and Seaside Drive emptied out at the lighthouse. Counting our house and the B&B across the street, we were pretty much the only houses in the area.

Meow!

I laughed. "Yes, I know you need food when we get home."

Meow!

"Yes, I got the brand you like."

Meow! Meow!

"Geez, Jinx! It happened *once!* One time in our nearly eighteen years together I messed up. When're you gonna let it go?"

Meow!

"Really? Never? You're such a man!"

Meeeeoooww!

I gasped. "Jinx O'Connell, we don't use that kind of language in this family."

I bent down to pick up the newspaper in our yard and then out of habit glanced over at the Copper Cove lighthouse. There was nothing but a hundred yard section of road and a field of weeds to the lighthouse.

Henley Waller was the lighthouse keeper and always had been as far as I knew. He was responsible for testing the ocean water around the lighthouse and making sure the place was kept up. In exchange he got to live inside. A pretty cool deal, I thought.

I hardly ever saw him around town except at the grocery store. Usually he just stood on the lookout on top of the lighthouse and watched the water. Just like I did when I sat on our widow's walk. Sometimes I'd take my binoculars off the water and use them to gaze over at him standing high in the air. More often than not, he looked so sad it nearly broke my heart.

I dug in my pocket and withdrew my key. I loved living just a stone's throw away from the ocean. The smell of the salty sea air, the noises from the seagulls and lapping waves...it all made me happy. What I didn't like was the lack of a social life. If this town grew about another hundred thousand people and there was something to do outside of counting the starfish and seashells along the shore, I'd never leave.

Grams' house was a three-story, seafoam green Victorian built on the edge of a steep cliff overlooking the ocean. When I was little, I used to get scared that the house would fall down the cliff and into the water. I still worried sometimes.

Our third floor was a large attic that was practically equal to the square footage of the downstairs. Grams had it packed full of antiques and boxes. The only time I went up there was when I wanted to sit on the widow's walk and daydream.

I breathed in the salty ocean air one last time before Jinx and I scurried up the three wooden porch steps.

"O'Connell family!"

I sighed and turned around. Peter Anders may not recognize me outside of the house, but I knew everything about him and his mean sister...even his smarmy voice.

"Mr. Anders," I said with a pretend cheerfulness I didn't feel.

He crossed the street in front of his sister's B&B.

"Imagine meeting you today," he said.

You pushed me aside an hour ago.

He stepped up onto the sidewalk in front of our house and then scrambled up the front steps. "I was just telling Milly I hadn't seen you or your lovely grandma in quite a while."

I glanced over and saw Milly on her front porch, rocking in her rocking chair. She was an odd one. Her place was usually full Tuesday through Sunday. Monday was the one and only day she closed down the B&B.

"What can we do for you, Mr. Anders?"

Meow!

Peter Anders glanced down at Jinx and blanched. Jinx was standing on his hind legs, swiping at the air and hissing.

18

"Um, yes. Well, I just wanted to leave my card with your grandma. Big developmental deal coming to Copper Cove shortly, and property values will soar. Your grandma may want to think about selling. I already have buyers lined up."

I laughed. No way would Grams ever sell her house. Our family was one of the founders of Copper Cove. And even if she *did* sell for some crazy reason, she sure as heck would never use Peter Anders to list. His sister *sued* Grams for pity's sake.

"I'll be sure and let Grams know," I lied.

I turned, unlocked the front door, and closed it in his face. He mumbled something under his breath about rude teenagers, but I really didn't care. He and his sister had caused Grams a lot of sleepless nights.

I bypassed the stairs and went to the kitchen to get Jinx some dinner. Once that was taken care of, I trudged up the stairs to my room. Flinging myself onto the bed, I laid there, prostrate, praying for something exciting to happen at the Copper Cove Festival.

CHAPTER 3

"I need to meet Peyton under the oak tree at seven," I told Grams as we walked toward the town park.

The park was a main hubbub in town. Not only did it have a place for kids to play, but there were also courts for basketball, tennis, and volleyball. To make sure everyone could have privacy, and to help reduce the noise level, each court was sectioned off with tall trees.

Tonight there were loads of booths and tons of food trucks set up all around the park. The familiar scent of hot buttered popcorn permeated the air, and my mouth watered. I was definitely getting popcorn before the night was over.

"You girls have fun," Grams said as she slipped me a couple bucks. "I'm going to meet up with Cheryl Potter. Be sure to keep your coat on, it's chilly tonight."

We split ways and went off in our own directions. I'd only taken a few steps inside the grassy park when someone pushed me from behind. I stumbled but quickly caught myself. I turned and glared at Seth Graham.

"Watch it," he said.

"Excuse me?" I asked. "I believe *you* pushed *me*. If anyone needs to watch it, it's you."

"That's enough, you two," Tara Graham said, staring down her nose at me. "I'm sure Brynn didn't mean to stop in front of you, Seth."

I rolled my eyes. It probably sounded like I had a huge chip on my shoulder, but people like Seth and his mom really pissed me off. How could she not see her kid was a major bully?

20

"I stopped by your grandmother's house this week and glanced through her garden," Tara Graham said, a fake smile plastered on her face. "I needed to see to some flora along the lighthouse coastline. Her culver's root looked good. As did her echinacea. I mean, for someone who never went to school to learn about cultivating and caring for such plants."

Nice backhanded compliment.

I gave her a fake smile in return. "Well, thank you. I'll be sure and tell her you said so. You being a learned woman and all, I'm sure she'll be impressed with your observation."

Tara Graham's phony smile fell from her face. "Your grandmother should be ashamed of herself. Raising you to be so disrespectful."

Seth snorted. "Yeah. Shameful."

I had two choices. I could either throw down and take them both on...or I could simply turn around and walk away. I *so* wanted to whip their pretentious snobby butts, but I knew Grams would just work herself up into a tizzy if I was taken into custody...again. For some reason, I had a habit of finding trouble.

Not *real* trouble. At least I didn't think so...but Chief Baedie thought differently. One time, I led a protest at the school over the lunches, and the next thing I knew, the principal called in Chief Baedie. Granted, the signs I made *may* have been a little over-the-top, but sometimes desperate times called for desperate measures. I was sure I learned that somewhere in one of my classes.

Without a word to either of them, I turned and continued my quest to find Peyton. I was still running through all the things I wished I'd said to Tara Graham and her bully son, when I practically clipped Mayor Barrow and a group of men. Mumbling an apology, I skirted around them. I recognized two city council members and Peter Anders. They were deep in conversation and paid no attention to me.

I stopped off at a food truck and bought popcorn and soda with the money Grams gave me. Sticking my tongue down in the bag to capture a popcorn kernel, I set out once again on my search for Peyton. I'd just spotted her leaning against a tree when I heard the unmistakable voice of Prudence Livingston.

"Take them both!" Prudence shouted as she shook the flyers she held in each hand. "Both are a nuisance to our town!"

"Great," I mumbled. "Now what's she up to?"

Being careful not to spill my precious popcorn and drink, I slid the popcorn bag down until it rested in the crook of my left arm and then clasped my drink with my left hand, leaving my right hand free. I scurried past Prudence, never made eye contact, and grabbed both flyers out of her hands without stopping. A few steps later, I slowed down and read the flyers. One was the same flyer she always handed out in front of Grams' shop touting the devil's work and witchcraft. The other flyer talked about the new plan the city was developing.

I read over the city development plan, because I already knew the lies she told about Grams' store. The city council was proposing to bring in a corporate conglomerate to build not only a hotel chain right at the city limits, but also a souvenir shop and restaurant.

22

I looked back over my shoulder, but didn't see Prudence anymore. I had no idea where she'd run off to.

"What took you so long?" Peyton sidled up next to me and snatched the popcorn out of my arms.

"Just reading this garbage Prudence is handing out. You see it?"

"Yep," Peyton said. "Same ole, same ole."

I drank in her long-sleeved, hip-hugging sweater dress, knee-high boots, curled hair, and grinned. "Nice. Guaranteed to get you a little attention."

"Think so?" Peyton asked hopefully.

"Trust me. If any guy gets a look at you in that dress, they'll—" I broke off and pointed as Prudence Livingston came into our view. "Wonder what she's doing back here?"

"Something on her phone definitely has her attention," Peyton said.

We watched as Prudence grinned, typed something, then ran toward a row of white fir trees.

"She's pretty excited to get behind those trees," I said.

"Do you know what she has against Granny Winnie?"

I shrugged. "No. And Grams won't tell me, either."

Peyton took a sip of my soda. "Hey, when I got home tonight I had another acceptance letter."

"Nice! What's that make now, seven?"

Peyton laughed. "Yeah." She sobered instantly. "But I'm only considering the same three you got into."

"Oh, Peyton," I shook my head. "You can pretty much go anywhere you want. Don't blow your chance because you want to go to college with me. You have big-name schools competing for you."

23

Peyton wanted to become a doctor. She just wasn't sure if it was for the living or the dead. She always thought she'd be a pediatrician...that is, until she recently started going out with her dad on calls, and now she was thinking more and more of becoming a medical examiner.

Peyton's dad owned the funeral home in town, and he was also the county coroner. She'd recently started going out and helping her dad when there was a death call, and she'd confided in me she liked it. And like me, she'd been getting a lot of pressure from her family about her future plans. Ultimately, her dad wanted her to take over the family business when he retired. But Peyton had been offered full-ride scholarships to big-name schools with great medical programs. Her mom and dad both encouraged her to go wherever she wanted, but I knew deep down when her schooling was over, her dad wanted her to come back to Copper Cove and run the funeral home.

"Isn't that the new girl Raven Masters over there?" Peyton suddenly asked.

"What? Where?"

"Over there." Peyton pointed to a cluster of trees some yards away. "It looks like she's going behind that same clump of trees Prudence went behind about five minutes ago."

"Why?" I asked.

Peyton grinned. "Let's go see."

Tossing another handful of popcorn in my mouth, I followed after Peyton. Truth was, I couldn't care less about Prudence or Raven. I was more worried about Peyton and her future plans.

"Back here," Peyton whispered.

I sighed and followed her behind the cluster of white fir trees, still chomping on my popcorn and sipping my soda. The tops of the trees cut off the glare of the street light, causing problems with visibility. Not a good sign for a clumsy girl.

"Raven should be right—oomph!"

"Ow!" I exclaimed, running into the back of Peyton. "Why'd you stop?"

"We've got a problem," Peyton said.

"Uh...you bet we do," I said to Peyton's back. "I just spilled some popcorn."

Peyton turned to me, her eyes wide behind her glasses. "We have more of a problem than your popcorn, Brynn. We have a dead body."

"What? Who's dead?" I poked my head around Peyton's back to try and see. Unfortunately, Raven Masters stepped in front of my line of sight.

"I found her this way," Raven said.

"Step back," Peyton said to Raven. "I have experience in these matters."

Raven snickered. "You touch a lot of dead bodies do you?"

Peyton ignored her and knelt down next to the body on the ground.

"Who is it?" I tried jockeying for a position so I could see, but between the lack of light and Peyton's tall form now kneeling over the body, I couldn't see anything.

Peyton stood up and brushed the grass off her knees. "It's Prudence Livingston. She's dead, and we are now contaminating the crime scene."

"Wha—what?" I asked. "Are you *sure*?"

Peyton sent me a get-real look. "Of course I'm sure. There's not a lot of light back here, but I believe I made out two puncture wounds. I'd say the killer stabbed her once in the sternum and then again an inch below that, this time leaving the murder weapon in her body."

"How could this—"

Peyton cut me off. "I mean, my dad will have to make the official pronunciation, but I'm telling you right now she's dead. The murder weapon was nice and sharp."

I turned to Raven. "What happened?"

Raven shrugged. "I don't know. I'd been watching her hand out flyers all night about Winnie's Apothecary. It really upset me. So I wanted to keep my eye on her."

"And what?" I asked. "You came back here and killed her?"

"Don't be stupid!" Raven hissed. "I came back here and found her like this."

"Did you see anyone chasing her back here?" I asked.

"No," Raven said. "She got a text, read it, replied, and then hurried behind these trees."

"That's pretty much what we saw," I said.

"When she didn't come back out," Raven continued, "I decided to see what was going on."

"I need to call Chief Baedie," Peyton said matter-of-factly as she tapped on her phone, "and report we have a dead body."

"And here I thought this new town was nice and quiet," Raven said.

26

I snorted. "It is. Nothing usually ever happens around here." I glanced down at Prudence's dead body now that Peyton had moved...and gasped.

"What?" Raven asked.

I was vaguely aware of Peyton still talking on her phone. Crouching down next to Prudence's body, my blood ran cold. "Give me a light."

Raven opened an app on her phone and flashed it down on me. I sucked in my breath. "This looks like one of Grams' stakes that was stolen out of her garden." I grabbed the phone and angled the light to the back of the nameplate sticking up from Prudence's chest cavity. "See. Grams' initials are on the back of the identification plate!"

"Oh no, Brynn," Peyton said, crouching down beside me. "And Prudence is still clutching one of those flyers she hands out about Granny Winnie's store."

"The nice lady that owns Winnie's Apothecary is your grandma?" Raven asked.

"Yes," I snapped.

I didn't mean to snap at her, but I was scared spitless. I may not be as smart as Peyton, but even I knew Grams was in serious trouble.

"Don't call the police," I said, hoping to stall the inevitable.

Peyton sighed. "Sorry, Brynn. I already did. I even told the dispatcher I thought it was Prudence Livingston. Plus I just sent my dad a text. It's only a matter of minutes now before this place is covered with cops."

"Pull the stake out of her chest and hide it," Raven said. "I won't say anything. I like Winnie."

My mouth dropped open. I wasn't sure if I was shocked at her declaration of Grams, or of her suggestion we cover up a murder. But I kind of admired her spirit. She may be weird, but she was also loyal.

"Do you guys see Prudence's cell phone?" I asked. "Because I don't."

Raven shone her flashlight app all over the ground, but we didn't see Prudence's cell phone anywhere.

"Do you think the killer took it?" Raven asked.

"What's going on?" a deep voice boomed before I could answer Raven. "You kids move aside."

I looked over my shoulder, and my heart fell to my stomach.

Chief Baedie was the last person I wanted to see. I'd already had a couple run-ins with him over the years. Mainly because he always seemed to be watching me like a hawk, waiting for me to mess up. He once gave Grams a ticket because I jaywalked in front of her store.

If I had to make a guess, I'd say he was about five foot six, two hundred eighty-pounds, and no matter the weather outside, he was always sweating. He liked to brag how Copper Cove was crime free because of him. I thought it had more to do with the fact the people of Copper Cove were good people. But after tonight, I was rethinking that.

He pushed me aside and knelt down. "Holy crap! It *is* Prudence Livingston! I thought the dispatcher was mistaken." A few seconds later he spoke into his walkie-talkie. "I have a dead body on the south side of the park behind a cluster of big bushes. I need an ambulance and the coroner, immediately."

28

"They're white fir trees," I said. "Not bushes."

Chief Baedie scowled. "I don't need your smart mouth, missy. In fact, why don't you go stand over there by those *white fir trees* and wait for my officers. For all I know, you're the one who killed her."

"Seriously?" I asked. "You think *I* killed her?"

"Where's Officer Casen?" Chief Baedie shouted into his walkie-talkie, ignoring my question. "I'm not getting any younger."

"I'm here." Tanner Patterson, Peyton's dad and the county coroner, knelt down next to Prudence's body. "And I just saw Officer Casen at his patrol car."

I grabbed another handful of popcorn and shoved it in my mouth. I was a nervous wreck now that the cops had made an appearance. How long before they noticed the murder weapon? Maybe they wouldn't put two and two together. I mean, Grams *did* file a police report on her stolen garden stakes, but maybe Officer Casen would forget he took down her statement at our house earlier this week.

Probably not.

"Sorry, Chief," Officer Casen said a few minutes later as he hurried over to the scene. "I was following up on something in my car."

Mr. Patterson stood up and sighed. "She's dead."

The chief let out a string of curses. I had to give him props...he knew how to curse.

I heard my name being called in the distance. I turned around and nearly wept at the sight of my Grams shuffling over to where we stood.

"Brynn!" Grams hollered. "Is that you?"

I tried to wave her away, but she wasn't having it.

"What're you and Peyton doing back here?" Grams asked.

"Go away," I hissed.

"Winnifred O'Connell." Chief Baedie ambled over to us, hands on his hips and a huge sneer on his face. "Just the person I was hoping to see."

"Why?" Grams asked.

"We got us a murder," Chief Baedie said, "and you're my number one suspect."

CHAPTER 4

"Chief Baedie, that's about the most ridiculous thing I've ever heard you say," Grams said. "And I've heard you say a lot of dumb things over the years."

I snorted. I couldn't help it. I got my love of sarcasm and smart mouth from her, no doubt about it.

"Now, who's dead?" Grams asked.

Chief Baedie sneered. "Like you don't know."

"Milton Baedie, you better start explaining yourself right now," Grams said, "or so help me I'll put a curse on you the likes you've never seen!"

I groaned. I *hated* when Grams did her pretend witchy thing. Like anyone here believed she could really curse people.

Chief Baedie and Officer Casen both took a step back, and I was shocked to see their eyes widen with fear. I never realized that it might just be *me* who thought Grams was harmless with her witchy spell speeches.

"It's Prudence Livingston," I said. "She's been stabbed. Murdered."

Grams' mouth dropped open. "Really? Pru, you say?" Her eyes narrowed on Chief Baedie. "I haven't seen Prudence tonight. I didn't even know she was here."

Chief Baedie snorted. "Likely story."

Officer Casen turned and listened as another officer spoke to him. I knew what that cop was telling Casen...that the stake sticking out of Prudence's chest had Grams' initials on it.

"Uh...Chief?" Officer Casen said. "Can I speak with you a minute?"

Chief Baedie tugged down his jacket over his wide girth, scowled once more at Grams, and headed over to speak to the other officers.

"Grams," I hissed. "Prudence was stabbed with one of *your* garden stakes that was stolen the other night. I saw it with my own eyes."

It was rare for my Grams to be left speechless, but I managed to do it with that declaration. "You're sure?"

"Yes," I insisted. "I'm really scared for you, Grams."

"We all are," Peyton said. "What should we do?"

Grams patted my arm, but I saw the slight tremor in her hand. "There's nothing to do. I didn't kill Prudence Livingston, so I have nothing to worry about."

I huffed. "You can't be—"

"Winnifred O'Connell," Chief Baedie said gleefully, "you need to accompany me back to the police station immediately."

"What for?" Grams said. "I didn't do anything."

"I'm not so sure about that," the chief said.

Grams waved her hand in the air. "Well, I am. Go look somewhere else for your killer."

A nasty-looking vein popped out on Chief Baedie's forehead. "We can do this the easy way or the hard way, Winnie." He reached back and pulled out a pair of handcuffs. "Either you go with me freely, or I take you down to the station cuffed and in the back of my patrol car."

Peyton, Raven, and I all three started yelling at Chief Baedie as he wiggled his handcuffs for show. Mr. Patterson hurried over and wrapped the three of us in his arms.

"You can't do this!" I cried. "She didn't do anything!"

"This is *so* not proper procedure!" Raven insisted. "Don't worry Miss Winnie, my dad will get you free!"

When I gave Raven a sharp look, she lifted her hands in the air. "I'll explain later."

"Girls, it's okay," Grams insisted. "Brynn, I need you to remain calm. I'll be home in no time."

Chief Baedie snorted. "Not if I have my way. You're going away for a long time."

"Grams, what do I do?" I didn't want to cry, but I could feel the tears welling up in my eyes.

By now a large crowd had gathered along the line of caution tape that blocked off the area. I had no idea when that had gone up. I recognized almost everyone standing there as Grams was led away through the crowd by Chief Baedie. Thankfully, he hadn't put the handcuffs on her.

"Brynn," Officer Casen said. "I need to take your statement. Do you have an adult family member who can sit with you?"

"Yes. But you just hauled her away in a cop car."

Officer Casen flushed. "She's just being questioned. Do you have a family lawyer who can sit with you?"

"No," I said.

"Yes," Raven said. "I just talked to my dad, Officer, and he said he'd meet you at the O'Connell house in half an hour."

"Your dad's a lawyer?" I asked.

I don't know why that shocked me. It just did. She didn't look like a lawyer's kid with her vampire-witch persona.

"Both of them are," Raven said nonchalantly. "But my dad's the one who's going to be able to help you."

"Why not your mom?" I asked.

"Because she's the district attorney for Mendocino County. She'll probably be prosecuting your Grams if it comes to it."

"Great," I said.

"Let me drive you girls to the house," Mr. Patterson said. "Get you out of this chilly air."

"Actually, Mr. Patterson, I'd rather walk," I said. "Clear my head a little."

"Yeah, dad. I'd like to walk with Brynn." Peyton looped her arms through mine. "Can you meet us at her grandma's house in thirty?"

Mr. Patterson leaned down and kissed Peyton's temple. "You bet, pumpkin."

He hurried back over to the body, and the three of us turned and walked back toward the park.

Meeeoow! Meow!

I blinked in surprise as Jinx sat grooming himself on a rock. "Jinx! What're you doing here? You're supposed to be home."

I swear the cat rolled his green eyes at me.

Meooow!

"I'm aware she's been arrested," I huffed.

Raven laughed. "Are you talking to that cat?"

34

"It's my cat," I said. "I've always had this weird connection to him."

I was about to go gather Jinx up off the rock when Henley Waller stepped out from nowhere. I nearly screamed. He didn't say anything, just stood there looking at me.

"Mr. Waller," I said. "I didn't expect to see you out tonight."

"What's going on with Winnie?" he asked.

I frowned. I wasn't even aware he knew my Grams' name. "Prudence Livingston was murdered tonight, and they think Grams did it."

His mouth dropped open. "Prudence Livingston is dead?"

"Yes," I said. "And they think Grams is the killer."

Mr. Waller's heavy brows furrowed. "That's ridiculous. Anyone who knows your grandma knows she'd never hurt another living soul."

"I know," I said. "But a few days back, someone took some of Grams' garden stakes out of her yard. And now it looks like one of them was used to kill Prudence." I leaned in closer to him. "Hey, you haven't seen anyone snooping around our place lately, have you?"

Mr. Waller slowly shook his head. "Can't say's I have."

A sudden thought occurred to me. Hadn't Tara Graham just admitted to me she stopped by to look at Grams' garden? Could she have stolen the stakes to kill Prudence? But why would *she* kill Prudence and try to pin it on Grams?

"Has Tara Graham been out to the lighthouse recently?" I asked him.

"Yes," he said.

"This week?"

He nodded. "Yes."

Good grief! Could you be any less forthcoming?

"Well, I need to get home," I said to Mr. Waller. "The police are coming by to take our statements since we're the ones who found Prudence."

"I'm real sorry you had to experience that," Mr. Waller said.

I shrugged. "Thanks, Mr. Waller. See ya around."

We waved goodbye, and I snatched Jinx up off the rock. Running at a near sprint, the three of us kept going and didn't stop to talk to anyone. By the time we reached Main and Ocean Drive, we were panting and gasping for breath. Dropping Jinx onto the sidewalk, I bent over and tried to suck in some much-needed air.

"Remind me not to wear a dress and boots the next time we find a dead body," Peyton said.

I laughed. "Yeah, that can't be comfortable to run in."

"C'mon," Raven said. "It will take them a while to get a search warrant for the rest of your Grams' garden stakes, but we don't want to leave your house unattended for long...just in case."

"You sure know a lot about this stuff," I said.

Raven shrugged. "Like I said, both my parents are lawyers. I've picked up a thing or two over the years."

"Do they want you to be a lawyer, too?" Peyton asked.

I almost laughed out loud at Peyton's question. I couldn't imagine Raven, with her purple hair and matching lipstick, standing in front of a jury in her all-black garb arguing a case.

"Let's go the back way home," I said.

We took a left on Ocean Drive so we could slip in through the garden. Winding our way down the sidewalk, I thought about who all might want to kill Prudence and pin it on Grams. When we got to the split in the road, we went right instead of going straight. Straight would take us to the Copper Cove pier and general store.

The only bad thing about going in the back way to Grams' house was the twenty steps you had to climb to get to the ridge where the house was built. Opening the gate, we quietly made the climb up the steps and through the enchanted garden my Grams was able to produce.

"I think they do," Raven said.

"Do what?" I asked.

"My parents want me to be a lawyer."

I'd forgotten Peyton had even asked the question.

"At least my mom wants it," Raven said. "My dad is cool with me doing whatever I want. My mom wants another attorney."

"Is that why you dress like that?" I asked. "Out of defiance?"

"Dress like what?" Raven deadpanned.

I snorted. "Good one."

She shrugged. "I don't know. Maybe. I honestly like the way I look and dress."

"Me, too," Peyton said. "I think the purple looks cool on you."

"Just promise me you don't sparkle in the sunlight," I joked.

Raven laughed and gave me a shove. "I don't sparkle, but I've been known to conjure up a spell or two."

"Then you'll fit in great around here," I mumbled.

I shook my head at the odd circumstances that led us to developing a friendship with Raven. Someone I never thought I'd be friends with. But under her crazy shock image she portrayed, she was smart, kind, and willing to commit a crime to make sure Grams didn't get blamed for something she didn't do. She was okay in my book.

"I don't know exactly when we noticed the stakes missing out of the yard," I said, "but it's only been a few days."

"You said a couple stakes were taken, right?" Raven asked.

"Yes," I said.

"That means someone in Copper Cove has more murder weapons," Raven said. "Because we only found one tonight."

"What do we do?" Peyton asked.

"Find the rest of the stakes and find the real killer," Raven said.

"How do we do that?" Peyton asked.

Raven grinned. "We do some sleuthing."

I frowned. "You mean *we* try and solve this crime?"

Raven nodded. "Yep. It's perfect really. No one will suspect three teenagers of trying to solve a murder."

I thought about what she'd just said. Could she be right? Could we really solve this case before the police?

"What do we know about solving crimes?" Peyton asked.

38

"Plenty," I said, surprising even myself with that answer.

Peyton looked quizzically at me.

"Peyton, you have medical knowledge, Raven has legal knowledge, and I have sheer desire *not* to see Grams thrown in jail."

I stopped and turned to the girls and stuck my hand out, palm down. Peyton and Raven quickly slapped their hands down over mine. "Right here, right now, we all agree to do whatever it takes to clear Grams."

"Let's do this!" Raven cried as we plunged our collective hands down in solidarity.

We walked up onto the front porch. Officer Casen's patrol car was in front of my house, but he was talking to Milly Anders across the street. He and Milly had been seeing each other for about a year now. When he caught sight of us, he gave Milly a peck on the cheek then jogged over to where we were.

"Let's get this over with," I said.

CHAPTER 5

Attorney Lowell Masters was a lifesaver. He showed up, assured me he'd already checked in on Grams at the station, and then gave Raven praise for bringing him up to speed on the investigation and possible incarceration of Grams. Basically treated her like an equal...like an adult.

It was always weird for me to witness other people's family dynamics. I'd never known what it was like to have a dad like Peyton and Raven. A dad who said he was proud of me. Heck, a dad who stayed around for me to even get to know. So having an adult male act like they were in awe of someone my age was a foreign concept.

But the two dads pulled it off tonight.

Mr. Patterson and Mr. Masters both insisted on staying and sitting in during our individual questionings. Raven's and Peyton's interview wasn't near as daunting as mine. While Officer Casen grilled me over and over again, both men flanked my side and didn't let Casen intimidate me. Because even though I thought I was tough enough to handle Officer Casen, I really wasn't. I just wanted my Grams. I just wanted this all to go away.

Officer Casen took me through the recent theft of Grams' stakes, the report she filed earlier in the week, and all the times Prudence had stationed herself outside Grams' store. He asked me about motives as to why Grams would kill Prudence. When I'd finally had enough and suggested Grams wasn't the only person Prudence was protesting, and maybe he needed to look into Mayor Barrow and some of the city council members, I thought Casen was going to stroke out.

"There is absolutely no reason for us to look at Mayor Barrow for this," Officer Casen said. "It's your grandmother's name on the murder weapon."

"How can you be so blind?" I asked. "I've told you a thousand times, obviously someone stole the stakes to frame her. Everyone knows that's how she marks the flowers in her garden. Always has."

And he knew it was true. Officer Casen had lived in Copper Cove for over twenty years. Grams' garden was a legend in the town. People wandered through it because they believed it held some sort of magical power. And because some plants were more dangerous than others, Grams labeled all her flowers.

"I'm telling you right now," I said, "the killer may very well be either Mayor Barrow or Tara Graham."

"Tara Graham?" Officer Casen asked. "You mean the county botanist? Why on earth would she kill Prudence?"

I rolled my eyes. "I don't know. That's your job. But I will tell you she confronted me tonight at the park and admitted she'd been on our property this week. She said Grams' flowers looked to be in decent shape."

"That's it? Because Tara Graham told you Winnifred O'Connell's flowers looked good, she's now the killer?"

"Why not?" I argued.

Officer Casen frowned. "I think I remember Tara Graham and Prudence Livingston both saying on more than one occasion that your grandma's store is a sham. That the herbs she sells don't help anyone. And if anyone would know, it's Tara Graham."

I pinched my lips together. "Grams' store is *not* a sham!"

Officer Casen asked and re-asked the same questions over and over again. And I had the same answers over and over again.

At ten o'clock, I finally closed the front door on him and leaned against it. I still hadn't had time to cry for Grams yet. I was fearful about how she was holding up. She wasn't exactly old, but she wasn't exactly young and agile, either. I couldn't imagine her having to sleep on a jail cell cot.

And that's exactly what was going to happen. According to Mr. Masters, when he'd called down to the station to check in on Grams a few minutes ago, he'd been informed that Grams had made a little spectacle of herself down at the station. So Chief Baedie said he was detaining her for twenty-four hours.

"You did great," Mr. Masters said as he buttoned up his coat. "Raven, do you want to catch a ride with me?"

Raven looked at Peyton then me. "Actually, Dad, Peyton and I were hoping to stay the night with Brynn and keep her company."

"I have no problem with that." Mr. Masters hugged Raven then opened the front door. "You got protection?"

I gasped. Was he asking what I thought he was asking?

Raven patted her front pocket then back pocket. "Knife and pepper spray handy."

"I can leave the flare gun if you want," Mr. Masters said.

Raven shook her head. "I don't think we'll need it." She turned to me. "I've also been studying Taekwondo since I was about eight. I'm a third level black belt."

"Get out!" Peyton said. "That's incredible."

"Brynn?" Mr. Masters laid his hand on my shoulder. "I'm heading down to the police station right now to be with your grandma."

"Thank you," I whispered.

"I already figured you'd want to stay the night," Mr. Patterson said to Peyton. "That's why I brought you an extra set of clothes for tomorrow."

Peyton grinned. "You know me well."

"I forgot your coat, so take my jacket in case you get cold tomorrow." Mr. Patterson shrugged out of his Patterson Funeral Home jacket and handed it to Peyton. "You girls be careful. Stay inside and lock the door behind us. We still have a killer on the loose." He leaned over and kissed Peyton's temple. "I just won't tell that last part to your mom when I see her."

Peyton smiled. "Thanks, Dad."

The two men hurried off to their cars, and I quietly closed and locked the door.

"A knife, pepper spray, black belt in Taekwondo, *and* flare gun if we needed it," Peyton said to Raven. "You really are a badass."

Raven gave a small bow.

Meow!

I picked up Jinx, rested my head against his tiny head, and let myself cry. Seconds later, I felt myself being hugged on each side by Raven and Peyton.

43

"We'll get through this," Peyton said. "Your Grams will be home tomorrow, and we'll get through this."

"We need to find the killer." I sniffed and wiped my eyes as Jinx jumped down. "Chief Baedie and Officer Casen both seem to already have their minds made up that Grams is guilty."

"Agreed," Raven said. "Starting tomorrow, Operation Save Winnie goes into effect."

Peyton laughed. "That's a great name."

"Speaking of great names," Raven said. "I was in the apothecary today after school and saw your soaps. I loved the clever names of some of them."

I'd spent a lot of time coming up with creative names like Purple Passions, Soothing the Savage Beast, and Lemon-Aid Lover. I used essential oils combined with flowers from Grams' garden.

"Thanks," I said. "She told me you recommended I put sage in the lavender and eucalyptus soap."

Raven shrugged. "I just thought it might be another great ingredient."

"You're right," I said. "It would be. That's the Soothing the Savage Beast. I also do it in a bath bomb, so it would definitely be a good idea."

Raven preened. "Thanks."

"Let's go to bed." I reached down and picked up Jinx. "I'm exhausted, and I'll need to open the apothecary by eight."

We trudged up the stairs, each lost in our own thoughts. I just hoped Grams was strong enough to last her night in jail.

44

CHAPTER 6

"That lousy, no good Milton Baedie wouldn't know a criminal if it came up and bit him on the butt!"

"Grams!" the three of us cried the next morning when she came barging into the apothecary proclaiming Chief Baedie's incompetency.

Meow! Meow!

We rushed her and smothered her in kisses and hugs.

"Are you okay?" I asked. "Did they hurt you? Did you get *any* sleep on that horrible cot you had to sleep on?"

Grams finished hugging each of us before pushing us aside and lifting Jinx up into her arms. "I'm fine. Just angry is all. How did you girls fare? I heard you all had a sleepover."

"We were just about to set up a board," I said. "Listing suspects and motives."

Grams frowned. "What for?"

Raven flipped her long purple hair back behind her shoulder. "Because like you said, the police aren't going to be of any help to you right now."

"I guess you might be right," Grams conceded.

I cleared my throat, prepared to broach a subject I knew she hated. "Grams, have you thought about contacting Aunt Aggie? She may be able to help us."

Grams scowled and fisted her hands on her hips. "No. Don't you even be thinking of calling her either, Brynn Leigh O'Connell. I won't have her here. She made the decision to leave Copper Cove over thirty years ago. Right when I needed her the most. Your Poppa had just died, and I had your momma to take care of on my own. And she up and abandoned me."

"Grams, you can't—"

"I said no."

Not that I had expected the conversation to go any differently. Grams and Aunt Aggie had been on the outs ever since Aunt Aggie left. I'd never met her, but I'd seen pictures of her in the albums Grams kept around the house. When they were young girls, they were inseparable. But when Aunt Aggie was in her late twenties, she left Copper Cove for San Francisco. And Grams never forgave her.

"But I heard you once say she did something in law enforcement," I said weakly.

Grams sniffed. "She captured bad guys who tried to run. That's not exactly law enforcement."

"Whoa," Raven said. "Like a bounty hunter? She's a bounty hunter?"

"*Was* a bounty hunter," Grams conceded.

"She might be exactly what we need," Raven said.

"No," Grams said stubbornly. "I won't call her. And don't you even think about it, Brynn. I mean it."

I sighed. "Fine. But you need to tell us the truth then, Grams. Obviously someone is trying to set you up to take the fall for Prudence's murder. You need to tell the truth as to who might hate you that much."

Grams averted her eyes. "I hear the police issued a search warrant this morning for the remainder of my garden stakes."

I sighed. It was going to be like pulling teeth when it came to getting information from Grams. "Yes. Mr. Masters accompanied the police to our house and went over the search warrant with me as they bagged up your garden stakes."

Grams' lips thinned and her chin quivered. "Did they trample on my flowers?"

"No," Raven said. "You'd have been proud of Brynn. She stood out there yelling at the officers, telling them they better watch where they were stepping or they'd regret it. It was awesome."

Grams gave me a side hug. "Thank you, Brynn. It nearly broke my heart when I thought about how careless they'd be. Those plants go into the remedies I give to help others."

The front door opened and Tabitha Cleary walked in. She waved and headed over, stopping every so often to sneeze and cough.

"Morning, Winnie," Tabitha said. "I'm so glad you're back in your place where you belong. I couldn't believe it when I heard the chief kept you overnight for questioning."

"Word travels fast," Grams said.

"You know it does in a small town." Tabitha sneezed and wiped her nose.

"Got yourself a cold?" Grams asked.

"Yes," she said. "I'm just miserable."

"Let me get you some of my homemade elderberry cough syrup and a package of honey and elderberry cough drops," Grams said. "You'll be feeling fine soon enough."

Grams wandered over to gather up Tabitha's purchases, leaving her in our company.

48

"No one really believes Winnie killed that troublemaker Prudence," Tabitha assured me. "Everyone I talked to today couldn't believe Winnie could do such a thing."

I swallowed past the lump in my throat. "Thanks."

"Here ya go." Grams bustled over and handed Tabitha her bag. "Now don't you worry, I just added it to your tab. The bill's going out sometime next week, so no hurry."

"Thanks, Winnie. You're a blessing to this community."

After Tabitha left, I grabbed a piece of paper and a pencil and got down to business.

"Grams, we've been talking, and we think since the killer took more than one garden stake, that maybe they intend to kill more than one person."

"Oh my goodness!" Grams exclaimed. "Do you really think so?"

Raven nodded, the tiny diamond in her nose twinkling. "Yes. I'd say it's highly probable that Prudence isn't the only one the killer wants to eliminate and pin on you."

"Why me?" Grams asked.

"You tell us?" I countered.

Grams averted her eyes. "I have no idea."

Liar. We'll do this your way, then.

"Outside of you," I said to Grams, "who else did Prudence fight with recently?"

Grams shrugged. "I don't know. Usually Prudence stationed herself outside of my store at least once a week for as long as I can remember, but I have no idea who else she fought with."

"We know there's Mayor Barrow," Peyton said. "You and I saw them exchanging some pretty heated words

49

yesterday after school. *Plus,* we both heard him threaten to kill her if she made trouble for him and the town council on this new land development deal."

Grams' mouth dropped open. "Mayor Barrow threatened to kill Prudence? Really?"

"Yes," I said. "Peyton and I both heard it."

"Did anyone else overhear the threat?" Grams asked.

I furrowed my brow. "I don't know. I don't think anyone else was around."

"What about that Peter Anders guy?" Peyton said. "Do you think he overheard?"

"Oh, yeah. That's right. He was walking toward us as we were passing the mayor and Prudence." I wrote down Peter Anders' name with a question mark. "I honestly don't know if he overheard or not. I guess we can ask him."

"I don't know about you girls getting involved," Grams said. "I want to say let the police handle it, but after last night I have my reservations."

"If you won't let me call in Aunt Aggie, then you're gonna have to be okay with us looking into this," I said. "Besides, Raven here is a woman with skills. She's got like a black belt and everything."

Grams raised an eyebrow at Raven.

"It's true," she said. "My dad wanted to make sure his little girl could defend herself if the time came."

"Smart man," Grams said.

"Who else might hate Prudence Livingston enough to kill her?" Peyton asked.

Grams sighed. "A lot of people. She was a menace in this town."

50

"Okay," I said. "Then let's talk about you. Why did Prudence hate you so much?"

Grams refused to make eye contact with me. Instead, she picked up a rag and started dusting.

"Grams, why you?" I pressed. "Why did Prudence hate you so much?"

Grams didn't say anything for a long time, just kept dusting. The other two girls shrugged, and I opened my mouth to remind Grams about truth telling when she finally broke her silence.

"It's silly really," she said. "It was such a long time ago, but she just couldn't let it go."

I laid my hand over hers. "What happened?"

"When your Poppa died, I was heartbroken. He was my world. Your mom was just a little girl, and I was still newly married for the most part. We'd been married just a little over eight years. Just a blip in the lifetime we were supposed to have together."

"What happened to your husband?" Raven asked.

"He was a fisherman," Grams said. "He went out early every morning and came in at dark. Such a hard worker." She wiped a tear from her eye. "But one night he didn't come home. A storm had come up suddenly, and he couldn't get in. They found his boat a day later, but never found him."

Peyton and I had heard this story a hundred times over the years. The grief Grams and my mother experienced.

"I paced my widow's walk for months, thinking I'd somehow get a miracle and he'd come sailing in and tell me a wild story about how he was carried out to sea but managed to survive." Jinx jumped up on the counter and nudged his head across Grams' face, offering comfort. She rubbed the top of his head absent-mindedly. "But I never got that miracle. My Charlie never came home."

"I'm so sorry," Raven whispered.

"That's the life of a fisherman," Grams said. "It's dangerous work."

"But what does that have to do with Prudence?" I asked.

Grams sighed. "Eight months later, I had a gentleman come to my door and ask me out."

"Okay?" I said. "And?"

"And this man had been dating a recently-divorced Prudence for about a year already. When word got around he'd asked me out, Prudence went ballistic."

My mouth dropped open. "I bet!"

"She did and said all sorts of terrible things," Grams said. "Both to me and this man."

"Why do you think he asked you out?" Peyton said. "If he was so taken with Prudence?"

Grams closed her eyes for a few seconds. "I'm not sure he was ever truly in love with Prudence. I think he just dated her because they were both single and Prudence had a little girl he liked, and..."

The three of us leaned in.

"And?" I prompted.

Grams sighed again. "And he was your Poppa's best friend. It made it easy for us to all hang out if he had a date."

I gasped. "What? The guy that ended up asking you out after Poppa died was his best friend?"

"Yes."

52

"Why haven't you ever told me this story before?" I asked.

"Because, Brynn, some moments are too private and personal to share."

"Wait." I held up my hand. "Did—do—I mean, did you *want* to date him?"

"It doesn't matter what I wanted," Grams said. "It could never be."

"Who is it?" Peyton's breath caught on her question, as though she was afraid to hear the answer.

"It doesn't matter," Grams insisted. "All you need to know is why Prudence Livingston hated me so much. Now you all know."

"Grams," I said. "Is this guy still around town? Does he live in Copper Cove?"

She shrugged. "Maybe."

"Maybe?" I said sarcastically.

She threw down the rag. "Fine. Yes, he does."

I threw my hands up in the air. "Grams, this could be a motive! Maybe this guy is the person who killed Prudence. Maybe he finally found a way to get back at Prudence and you for rejecting him!"

I could feel myself shaking, excited at the possibility that we'd already solved the case.

"It wasn't him," Grams simply said.

"How do you know?" I argued. "You act like you haven't seen him in all these years. Maybe he's changed. Maybe he became a crazy hermit who finally snapped and got revenge."

"I never said I didn't see this man anymore," Grams hedged.

I threw my hands up in the air again, totally exasperated with Grams. "Okay. I'm done with the riddles. Who is it? Who was Poppa's best friend that wanted to date you after he died?"

Grams pursed her lips together. "Henley Waller."

CHAPTER 7

"What?" I yelled. "The man who practically lives next door from you, in a lighthouse, is your secret love?"

"He's not my love," Grams said. "Your Poppa was my love. Henley was only a friend."

"Then why do you go out of your way to avoid him?" I asked. "I always thought you didn't like him for some reason. That's why you avoid him."

Grams scowled. "Do you know how bad it would have looked if I'd have dated your Poppa's best friend after he died?"

"Actually," I said, "you might be surprised how *not* bad it would have looked. I bet a lot of people would have understood."

Grams pursed her lips but said nothing.

"He was at the park last night," I said, hoping to throw her off her game. Shake her up a little.

"What?" Grams asked. "He was?"

"That's right," Peyton said. "We spoke with him."

"He was right there next to Jinx," I said. "Both of them practically appeared out of nowhere. He asked what happened, and when I told him you'd been detained for possibly killing Prudence Livingston, he said no one in their right mind would ever believe you could hurt someone on purpose."

"He did?" Grams asked.

I could tell she was pleased.

"I also asked him if he'd seen anyone sneaking around our place. He said he hadn't."

Maybe I needed to have another meeting with Mr. Waller. Find out his true feelings about Grams. Could he have held onto a grudge all these years and finally acted upon it? Or did he truly care for Grams even after all these years?

"Let's get back to the other motives," I said. "We know why Mayor Barrow would want Prudence dead, so he's definitely a suspect. I saw him at the park last night, so he could have killed her."

"Who else?" Raven asked. "Because right now we have a suspect list of one person."

I groaned and plunked my head down on the counter. This was a lot harder than I thought it was going to be.

"Wait!" I lifted my head. "I can't believe I forgot this. Tara Graham. She also cornered me at the park last night and made some snide comment about some of your plants looking good, Grams. She admitted to being at our place earlier this week!"

"So now all we have to do," Peyton said, "is figure out why Tara might want to kill Prudence and blame it on your Grams."

We were silent, casting furtive glances at Grams, wondering if she'd give us something. When she didn't say anything, I decided to press on.

"I don't know enough about the two women to even fathom a guess," I said. "Did they even know each other?"

"I'm sure they know each other," Grams said. "Tara Graham and the mayor's wife, Lillian, are best friends."

"And?" I asked. "Why does that mean anything?"

Grams looked at me funny then smiled. "I forget sometimes you girls don't know about the lives of others in this community. They would know each other because Lillian Barrow is Prudence's daughter. She used to be Lillian Livingston."

"What!"

"No way!"

"How did we not know this!"

The three of us shouted and hollered at Grams. She started to laugh. "Oh, you girls. I needed that laugh."

"You're saying Mayor Barrow *threatened to kill* his own mother-in-law?" I demanded. "That's what that means?"

Grams shrugged. "Seems that way from the story you're telling me. You said he told Prudence to back off or he'd kill her. That seems to me to be a mother-in-law threat."

"This is too bizarre," Peyton said. "The scandal."

"Okay," I said. "So we know that Tara Graham knows Prudence, but why would she want to kill her and make it look like you did it?"

"You got me," Grams said.

"Aren't we missing something important and obvious?" Peyton said.

"What's that?" I asked.

"The person who killed Prudence may have gotten blood on them. I mean, they stuck her twice. I'm assuming it's because they wanted to make sure the blood pumped out of her quickly. I don't think there'd be arterial spray or anything, but there might be at least some blood splatter."

I crinkled my nose. "Gross."

Peyton shrugged. "But true."

"So what're you saying?" I asked Peyton.

"Maybe we need to look in Mayor Barrow's and Tara Graham's garbage cans," she said. "Just in case they threw out the clothes."

"You think they'd be that stupid?" Raven asked.

"I think they probably know that the police are pretty much only looking at Granny Winnie," Peyton said. "The mayor and the chief are close friends. Believe me, if the mayor is involved, it'll be up to us to prove it."

"Okay then," I said. "I think we know what we need to do next. But I think we also need to check the park. Maybe after one of them stabbed Prudence, they didn't have enough time to go back to their car and hide the jacket they were probably wearing since it was cold last night. Maybe they hid the jacket around the crime scene."

"Did any of you notice if either the mayor or Tara were missing their coats?" Grams asked.

"I was so shocked about Prudence," I said, "I don't even really remember seeing either of them after the body was discovered."

I looked at Peyton and Raven, but they shook their heads.

"I don't remember seeing them, either," Peyton said.

"I don't even really know what this Tara Graham looks like," Raven added.

I clapped my hands together. "Okay. We know our next move. Let's get movin'."

Grams sighed. "Please be careful."

I gave her a peck on the cheek. "I promise."

58

The doorbell jingled, and I figured that was the perfect excuse for us to sneak away and start snooping for the killer. Waving goodbye to Grams, we hurried out of the shop.

"Who first?" I asked.

"I think Mayor Barrow is our best bet right now," Peyton said. "I mean, you and I heard him threaten Prudence with our own ears. I think he should be our number one suspect."

"Works for me," Raven said. "How about we stop by my house real quick, and I'll grab the keys to my car."

"You have your own car?" I asked.

Having a car wasn't exactly a necessity in Copper Cove. You could get all the way across town in under twenty minutes just by walking.

"Technically, it's a hand-me-down," Raven said. "I think, like, my great-great grandfather drove it or something."

My mouth dropped open. "Wow! Really?"

"What is it?" Peyton asked.

"A '66 Mustang Fastback," Raven said.

I counted back in my head. Probably not her great-great grandfather, but I bet it was something like that. It seemed old anyway.

"Is it reliable?" I asked. "Seems to me something that old would break down a lot."

Raven shook her head. "My dad insists older is better." She shrugged. "Must be an adult thing. It's cool, though. My dad used to drive it when his dad passed it to him. And now I get to take it out whenever I need to." She gave us a wicked grin. "It's really, really fast."

We crossed the street and decided to make a pit stop at Sisters to grab coffee and chocolate croissants. The place was packed with locals all talking about Prudence's murder.

"Did Winnie break free this morning?" Jessica asked as she handed me my mocha with an extra shot.

"She did," I said. "Mad as could be."

Janice tsked. "I heard there's some pretty hard evidence against her. Some kind of giant scissors that had her name on it or something?"

I took a sip of my coffee. "Someone broke into Grams' garden and stole her special garden stakes. The smaller ones she uses for her herbs in the pots."

"What's this town coming to?" Susan Ghatto said behind me. "While I'm not shocked Prudence Livingston was murdered, I'm offended your grandmother would kill her at the park where others were trying to have a good time."

I turned around slowly, my brain trying to process what Susan was saying. "You honestly think my Grams could kill Prudence? Really?"

Susan averted her gaze. "It's not my place to say whether or not she did, I'm just saying she should have done it somewhere else."

I growled low in my throat.

Peyton grabbed my arm. "Let's go. We don't need you getting arrested, too."

We'd just made it to the door when Shelly Vogel stopped me. "Pay Susan no mind. Everyone knows if your grandmother was going to kill someone, she'd do it with those witchy herbs and poisons she uses in her shop."

"What the—"

"Thank you for your kind words, Mrs. Vogel," Peyton said, pushing me out the door.

"Kind words?" I grumbled as we continued walking down Main Street. "Has everyone gone mad?"

"They just don't understand what your Grams does, that's all," Raven said. "The minute something bad happens, it's natural for people to blame what they don't understand. People like your Grams have been persecuted for centuries for using herbs and flowers and natural elements to help cure people. Look at the Salem Witch Trials."

I stopped and stared at Raven. Really took her in. She was dressed in the same black jeans, black sweater, and black boots as yesterday since she stayed overnight. She'd pulled back her purple locks into a quick ponytail, but she still had on her matching purple lipstick and nose ring. I had made certain assumptions about her based on her appearance alone. Judged her and made fun of her. Just like other kids did to me. In truth, I was no better than my peers who poked fun at me because *I* was different.

"Thank you. I seriously owe you an apology. When you first got here a couple weeks ago, I made assumptions about you that weren't true. And here you are, not knowing anything about my family, willing to help out. Thank you."

Raven cocked an eyebrow, a twinkle in her eye. "What sort of assumptions about me?"

Peyton laughed. "C'mon you two. We have clues to find today."

Five minutes later we were walking up the driveway to Raven's house.

"I didn't realize you bought the old Crandall place," I said.

"Pretty awesome, huh?" Raven asked.

"Pretty creepy," Peyton mumbled.

The old Crandall place had been abandoned for years. When I was in second grade, the owners, Bob and Norma, had been in their backyard enjoying their hot tub when a lightning bolt struck their tub. The two were killed instantly. Years later the house was sold to a woman who died inside from a slip and fall. Her bathtub had overflowed, and when she tried cleaning it up, she fell and hit her head against the side of the toilet.

If you could get past the cursed factor, the house was pretty incredible. The two-story old Crandall place was neon chartreuse green with canary yellow shutters. The only neutral part of the house was the white spindles attached to the wide front porch.

"Mom hates it," Raven said. "But dad loves it."

"Why'd you move here?" I asked.

Raven shrugged and pushed open the front door. "The town of Ukiah is actually pretty cool, but Mom and Dad couldn't escape their jobs working in the same town they lived in. Plus Dad just wanted something different for me."

"Your dad is pretty amazing," I said.

And yes, I heard the envy in my voice.

Raven shrugged. "They're both all right. For parents. A little weird most times. They like to think they're still young, especially my dad. He dances around in the kitchen and tries to get my mom to join him, he tells the dumbest dad jokes, and most nights they can't stay up past ten o'clock."

I sighed. I thought it sounded wonderful.

Peyton must have heard the wistfulness in my sigh because she reached over and slipped her hands through my arms.

CHAPTER 8

"Raven Delilah Masters," a woman's voice called out. "Is that you?"

Raven rolled her eyes and sighed. "Yes, Mom. Just stopping by to get the keys to the Mustang."

A tall, willowy woman with chin-length black hair cut in a bob stepped into the foyer. She cradled a cup of coffee in her bony hands and leaned against the doorjamb.

"Who're your friends? I'm assuming one of them is the granddaughter of the woman your father is helping?"

Raven threw up her hand. "Mom, this here is Brynn O'Connell. Her grandma is the one the police are looking at for the murder. They own that cool apothecary on Main Street."

I was afraid she'd be mad at Raven for bringing me into the house and demand I leave. When she didn't say anything, I gave her a tentative smile. She looked like she could eat someone like me for breakfast and clean her teeth with my bones. No wonder she was a successful lawyer.

"And this is Peyton. Her dad is the coroner in town. He came out last night and made the official pronouncement. I mean, after Peyton did it first."

Mrs. Masters' eyes cut sharply to Peyton and she looked her up and down. I barely tamped down on the urge to hold Peyton's hand out of fear.

"That was quick and rational thinking on your part to check over the body and call the cops," Mrs. Masters said. "It couldn't have been easy."

Peyton shrugged. "I want to be a doctor. I just don't know if I want to work on live people or dead people yet."

Mrs. Masters nodded and took a sip of her coffee. "We're hoping when the time comes Raven will want to follow in our shoes." Before Raven could argue, her mom turned and looked at me. "And you? What are your plans after you graduate in May?"

I almost snorted. I was sandwiched between a wanna-be doctor and wanna-be lawyer. How could I compete with that? I wanted to make people look good on the outside. Make them feel good about themselves. It sounded shallow.

"I don't know," I mumbled. "I think I'd like to get a degree in pharmaceuticals."

I didn't elaborate on the emphasis in cosmetics.

Mrs. Masters smiled, and it changed her whole face. "Bright futures. You girls should be proud."

"So," Raven said, "can I take the Mustang?"

"Take the Mustang?" Mr. Masters' voice boomed as he walked down the stairs. "What's on the agenda for today? Are you girls snooping around?"

"I don't know why you encourage her so," Mrs. Masters said, scowling at Raven's dad.

He grinned, walked over to his wife, and kissed her on the temple. "Because she needs to learn problem-solving skills."

I liked him so much.

"Hey, Raven, what do you call a fake noodle?" Mr. Masters asked. "An impasta!"

He threw back his head and laughed at his own joke.

Raven snickered. "Lame, Dad."

Mr. Masters winked at me. "I got a million of them if you want to hear more?"

Yes.

"No." Raven grabbed our arms and propelled us toward the back of the house. "We have to go. Thanks for letting me use the Mustang."

"Be careful," Mrs. Masters yelled.

"Have fun," Mr. Masters countered.

Raven grabbed a set of keys off the kitchen counter and motioned us to follow her. A two-door, two-toned red and white Mustang was parked in the center of the garage. It was so shiny I could see my face in the panel.

"Mom and Dad park their cars in the carriage house out back."

I ran my hand lightly over the glossy door. "It's pretty."

"Hop in," Raven said. "Let's go."

Peyton scurried around the hood and nabbed the front seat. I opened the car door but just stood there. I'd never ridden in a two-door car before. There didn't seem to be a lot of room for me to get in.

"Do I just jam my body back there?" I asked.

Raven laughed. "No."

She reached in and pushed the top half of the seat forward so I had a little more room to squeeze in. I slid in the back, positioning myself in the middle of the seat so I was situated between the two of them.

"It's so different from a normal car," I said. "That's a pretty crazy wheel." The steering wheel was circular like a regular car, but shooting from the middle were three skinny, metal bars. "Where's the horn?"

66

"Right here." Raven reached over and pushed a button on the dash.

Peyton and I both screamed as the garage echoed with the reverberations from the horn.

"Dad redid the exhaust last year so it wouldn't kill my eardrums," Raven said as she started the car. "You should have heard this thing years ago. For days I couldn't hear after riding around with Dad."

"I'll pull up the police scanner so we can know what's going on." Peyton pulled her phone out and swiped until she came to the Copper Cove Police app.

"You have that app on your phone?" I asked. "Why?"

"I have one, too," Raven said. "But mine's still programmed into Ukiah's police station. Who knew Copper Cove was so lit?"

Not me.

"Do we have any idea how we're going to get inside the mayor's house to dig through his trash?" Peyton asked.

"I've been thinking about that," I said. "And I think I've come up with a plan. Peyton, text your dad and see if the mayor and his wife are at the funeral home meeting with your dad to go over arrangements."

While Peyton texted her dad, I had Raven make a pit stop at the floral shop. After plunking down hard-earned soap money I'd grabbed before leaving the house, I filled them in on what I was thinking. I then gave Raven directions to the mayor's house while Peyton got ready.

By the time we pulled up in front of Mayor Barrow's house, Peyton had her hair pulled back in a sophisticated knot, her dad's Patterson Funeral Home jacket on, and my plan cemented in her brain.

"Here, put these on." Raven grabbed a pair of oversized sunglasses from the glovebox and handed them to me. "It'll help hide your identity."

I shoved the glasses on my face. "Peyton, your dad told you the Barrows were at the funeral home. As far as anyone answering the door is concerned, we're just making a delivery to the grieving family."

"Usually we don't deliver flowers to the family until *after* the funeral," Peyton pointed out.

"No one is going to know," Raven said. "It's actually a brilliant plan."

I preened a little at the praise. I may not be doctor or lawyer smart...but I was pretty street smart when I needed to be.

I lifted the huge vase of flowers I was carrying in front of my face and held my breath as Peyton shifted her smaller vase to knock on the front door of the mayor's house. A few seconds later, a middle-aged Hispanic woman opened the door and ushered us inside.

"Flowers already?" she asked. "Let me go grab a small table from another room so we can display them here in the foyer."

I groaned. I needed to at least get to the kitchen and look through the trash. I had to find something that would get Grams off the hot seat. Because the way I saw it, Mayor Barrow *had* to be the killer. I'd heard him threaten to kill Prudence if she didn't stop making waves for the city council, *and* he was at the park last night.

68

According to Peyton, it wouldn't have taken more than a few seconds to stab her, and then a few minutes for her to bleed out. Giving him plenty of time to stash his jacket either in the park or in his car.

"Here we are." The housekeeper dragged in an antique table and shoved it against the wall.

"Thanks," Peyton said. "We're working overtime today because of the death."

The housekeeper clucked her tongue. "That poor woman. I heard Mrs. Barrow crying this morning saying her Madre had been killed by a spear in the throat. Can you imagine?"

I didn't correct her on her mistake.

"Could I have a drink of water?" I asked. "I'm really thirsty."

The housekeeper scrunched her nose and looked like she was about to say no.

"And could I use your restroom?" Peyton asked. "Like I said, so many deliveries being made today we haven't had time to take a break."

The housekeeper sighed impatiently and gestured down the hall. "Restroom down there. You come with me. I get you drink. Then you leave."

I followed the housekeeper to the back of the house. It wasn't like I expected to see Grams' stakes or his bloody clothes sitting out. That would be an obvious no-no on the mayor's part, but maybe I could find something.

The woman handed me a glass of water, and I slowly walked around the kitchen as I sipped. I could tell by her constant sighing she was growing impatient, but I couldn't see a trash can anywhere. That left under the sink.

In the distance I heard the toilet flush. I knew I had to act now. As casually as possible, I walked over to the sink and opened the doors underneath.

"What are you doing?" she huffed.

"Oh," I said, pretending to be startled. "Silly me. I thought I was putting the glass in the sink."

"I thought I should tell you there wasn't any toilet paper in the bathroom," Peyton said from the doorway.

The housekeeper frowned. "How can that be? I just restocked yesterday."

As she huffed her way out of the kitchen, I dropped the glass in the sink and yanked the trash out from under the counter. Suppressing the urge to gag, I quickly dug down as deep as I could, hoping a jacket or something would be at the bottom.

Nothing.

"What're you doing?" The woman's scream jerked me upright, causing me to spill some of the trash on the floor.

"Sorry." I bent to pick it up. "I washed my hands and went to throw away the paper towel. You startled me."

She narrowed her eyes. "That is not what it looked like."

I shoved the trash can back under the sink, rewashed my hands, and then dried them on my pants. "Thanks for the water. Give our condolences to the Barrows for us."

I grabbed Peyton's arm, trotted to the front door, and then sprinted to the car...Peyton close behind.

"Anything?" Raven asked.

"Nothing," Peyton said. "I even gave Brynn some extra time by hiding the toilet paper when I went to the bathroom."

I laughed. "Is that what you did? That's funny. She's going to be mad when she finds it one day."

"Did you see anything?" Raven asked me.

"No. I dug through the trash to the bottom and everything."

"I'm sorry," Peyton said. "I was hoping we'd find something this first time out."

I sighed. "It's okay. We still have one more stop."

"Botanist chick's place?" Raven asked.

"Yeah," I said. "Tara Graham. She has a son in our class."

"Huge bully," Peyton added. "Seth Graham. Have you met him yet?"

Raven made a vomiting noise. "Brown hair, drives a convertible, thinks he's God's gift to women?"

"That's him," I agreed.

"Know him well. He's tried hitting on me, threatening me, making fun of me. All in the hopes I'll go out with him." She snorted. "He says it's my right as the new girl to get to date him."

Peyton shuddered. "That's just wrong."

"I don't know how we're gonna get in yet," I admitted.

Raven shot Peyton and me a quick smirk. "I've got that covered."

One good thing about living in a small town your whole life, you pretty much knew where everyone lived. The Graham house was just a little past the outskirts of town where the terrain was more level. About ten years ago a developer built a small subdivision of eight houses out in the middle of nowhere. At least that's how it seemed to me.

Raven pulled the Mustang over and dug out her cell phone. "Okay, I have his social media pulled up. I'm going to direct message him and see if I get a response."

Ten seconds later, Raven's phone beeped.

"I'm in," she said. "I told him I have my dad's '66 Mustang Fastback out today and wanted to know if he'd like to go for a ride."

I looked at Raven and frowned. "You don't have to do this."

"Do what?" Raven asked.

"Be alone with him," I said. "It isn't worth the risk."

Raven laughed. "Do you forget I carry around a knife and pepper spray. He makes one slimy move on me, and he'll be missing some vital organs."

I grinned. "Okay then."

Raven's phone beeped again. "What a scumbag. Although good for us. He just told me his mom is at the vet with their dog, so after the ride I can come in and he'd show me around."

I shivered. "Please be careful, Raven."

"I will."

"I say we get out here and walk the rest of the way to his house," Peyton said. "Maybe there'll be a door or something open."

"If not," Raven said, "it's pretty easy to pop out a screen and jump in a window."

"Who *are* you?" I mused.

Raven laughed. "A girl needs to be prepared at all times."

Peyton and I cut through a side yard as Raven drove to the house I'd pointed out was Seth's. As she pulled into the driveway, he walked out of his house. We scrambled through his neighbor's backyard, and I tried to listen in on what he was saying.

"Nice ride," he said. "Maybe I should drive."

Raven laughed. "Nice try, slick. Get in if you want to go."

"Let me lock the front door real quick," Seth said.

"Last chance," Raven said as she got in the Mustang and started to back out slowly. "You either come now or not at all."

Well played, Raven!

"I'm coming," Seth said as he jogged over to the passenger side.

Raven squealed out of the driveway and took off like a rocket down the street.

"Let's go," I said.

CHAPTER 9

The inside of the Graham house was spotless and smelled faintly of disinfectant. Almost like a germ-free lab. The walls were white and bare, and the white tiled floor seemed cold and sterile.

"Oh, this is nice and cozy," Peyton joked.

I snickered. "You check the kitchen, and I'll run upstairs and see if I find anything in Tara's bedroom and bathroom."

I took off up the stairs, two at a time. I had no idea obviously which room would be hers, but I didn't think it would be too hard to find.

I peaked in the first door and came across Seth's bedroom. The rest of the house may be spotless, but in here he was a normal teenager. He had dirty clothes and dishes spread around his room, and a laptop and gaming system sat on his unmade bed.

The next door in the hallway was a bathroom. It, too, was pristine white. Figuring the last door to be Tara's bedroom, I jogged to the end of the hall.

Tara Graham's bedroom was just like the rest of her house—sterile with a touch of lonely. Her bed was made, no clothes were thrown on the floor, and all her bottles were neatly lined up on her dresser. If this was what adulthood was supposed to be like, don't sign me up. I'd rather go kicking and screaming than to conform to this idea of perfection.

It was obvious there was no bloody coat or clothes hanging around, but just to make sure, I tiptoed to her bathroom off of the bedroom. No surprise, gleaming floors and walls, cosmetics nice and neat—which I begrudgingly admired—and even her toilet seat was down.

Nothing.

Nothing that led me to believe that she stuck a twelve-inch garden stake in Prudence Livingston's chest.

I jogged back down the hallway, down the stairs, and had just made a beeline for the kitchen when I heard voices on the front porch.

"You broke my nose!" Seth cried.

"Serves you right for trying to get handsy," Raven said.

The front door cracked open.

Oh, crap!

I took off toward the kitchen and had just rounded the corner when I ran smack into Peyton.

"Look how cute," she said. "They have one of those doggie walls so their dog can go outside even though there's no door back here."

My hands were waving frantically in the air, but I couldn't help it. "Go! Go! We have to leave. They're coming inside!"

"Where? There's no back door!"

I could hear footsteps on the tile floor heading our way.

Peyton snatched my hand and yanked me down to the ground. "Follow me."

She crawled on her hands and knees toward the doggie door in the wall of the house. Why the heck these people couldn't have a door in their kitchen like the rest of the world I had no idea.

I watched in complete horror as Peyton shot her skinny little body out the tiny door. Okay, it wasn't exactly tiny. In fact, if I had to guess, I'd say the family dog was a pretty good sized dog. But still, I was pretty sure I couldn't wiggle my way through a doggie door.

"Where're you going?" I heard Raven scream.

I almost answered her. I thought she was yelling at me.

"In the kitchen to get some ice for my nose," Seth said. "You need to leave."

"Psst," Peyton hissed through the open flap. "Get out here!"

Knowing I had no other choice, I flattened myself on the ground, hands out in front of me, and started wiggling my way out the tiny door. I was doing good, too, until my lower half tried to fit.

"Crap," I hissed. "I'm stuck!"

Peyton grabbed hold of my arms and started yanking, stretching, and pulling my arms out of my sockets.

I heard Raven scream from inside the kitchen.

"What?" Seth asked. "Geez, now you busted my eardrum on top of giving me a bloody nose. What the heck is wrong with you?"

In times of extreme duress...I laugh. I can't help it, it's just who I am. In that moment I pictured Raven witnessing my butt and legs wiggling through an opening in a wall, while Peyton was in front of me acting like I had elastic in my arms.

I lowered my head toward the ground and snorted.

"Brynn O'Connell, don't you dare go into hysterical laughter right now," Peyton said. "You'll give us away."

I giggled. "More like my butt is going to give us away."

I could hear muffled voices talking in the kitchen, but figured I was safe since no one was yanking on my legs like Peyton was yanking on my arms.

Peyton finally let go of my arms, grabbed me around my chest, and tilted me up on my side. I was now facing the neighbor's house. Thank goodness no one was out in the backyard watching this. With one more good yank, my lower half slid out and Peyton and I fell to the ground.

"You okay?" Peyton asked.

"No," I said. "I think you pulled both arms out of their sockets, *and* I'm sure I have scrapes and scratches all along my side."

"Don't be a baby," Peyton said.

We slowly got to our feet but stayed crouched down so we couldn't be seen from inside. I still couldn't believe we hadn't gotten caught. How did Seth not hear the swish of the dog door when I popped out?

"What're you two doing?" Raven hissed from the side of the house. "Let's go!"

I stared open-mouthed at her. "How did you get outside so fast?"

"I'll explain in the car," she whispered. "Let's *go!*"

Peyton and I popped up and took off after her. She had her driver's side door open and the seat down, so I didn't have to slow down as I dove head-first into the backseat.

Two seconds later we were squealing down the road screaming our lungs out in both fear and excitement. Raven pulled over at the entrance to the housing development and rested her head on the steering wheel.

"What the heck happened?" I asked.

Raven lifted her head. "So we're driving along, and the little worm decides to get handsy with me. I gave him a warning. When he tried it again," she lifted her fist in the air, "I gave him a little tap to the nose."

I threw my head back and laughed.

Peyton looked impressed. "That had to be some hit to the nose."

"Not really," Raven said. "Not if you know what you're doing. You want to hit the side of the nose. The side will give you the biggest bang for the buck, unless you hit *under* the nose and go upward. That hurts, too."

Peyton grinned. "You can shoot a gun, maim a person without breaking a sweat, *and* you drive a cool car. You're like a superhero."

I reached up and gave each girl a high-five. "That was probably the craziest thing I've ever done. But thrilling, also."

"Did you get anything?" Raven asked.

My high came crashing down. "Nothing upstairs. No traces of blood, no bloody clothes, no extra stakes. Nothing."

"Me, either," Peyton said. "Nothing in the trash cans."

"Now what?" Raven asked.

"Let's go to Grams' and grab some lunch," I said. "Maybe something will come to us there."

I leaned back in the seat and closed my eyes. I had no idea where to go from here. My two main suspects had nothing on them that could be connected to Prudence's murder.

Raven pulled up in our front driveway, and I waited patiently for her to fold the seat down before crawling out of the back seat. As I stood up, I saw Milly Anders rocking on her front porch, staring at us.

I waved. We may not be her favorite people, but I had to wonder if maybe she hadn't seen someone rummaging around our place lately. She always seemed to have her hawk eyes on us.

"Let's go see Ms. Anders real quick," I said.

We jogged across the road and up her front steps. She never once stopped rocking. I put her around forty, but one thing about older people, I can never really guess their age right. To me, anyone over twenty-five is pretty old. Grams said when I finally got to be twenty-five, I was going to laugh at that absurd thought. But right now, it was true.

She wasn't as old as Grams, but she wasn't twenty-five, either. She was on the tall side for a girl, kinda like Peyton. But whereas Peyton was skinny, she was also healthy. Milly just looked sickly and waiflike. Her mousy brown hair was pulled back in a low ponytail, and her eyes always looked sunken in. A brown cardigan was wrapped tightly around her body, and I could just make out a brown and white dress underneath.

Seaside Bed and Breakfast sat less than one hundred yards from the lighthouse and overlooked the ocean. No matter what she claimed, her guests had a clear view of the water.

Milly and her brother had moved to Copper Cove five years ago when she bought the Bed and Breakfast and he opened a real estate office. I knew from town gossip that they both used to live in Sacramento. I never did understand why Peter Anders would leave a bigger city to try and make a living in our small town. But he seemed to be doing well enough, especially if the town decided to start building more. More jobs, means more people, means more houses. I'm pretty sure I learned that in my economics class.

"Hello, Ms. Anders," I said. "Sure is a nice day."

She stopped rocking. "Is it? I don't know. I can't really tell with that big obstacle in front of me."

Well, so much for pleasantries.

"I was wondering if you could tell me whether or not you've seen someone snooping around our place lately? Maybe in Grams' garden?"

"I heard your grandmother killed Prudence Livingston last night," Milly said.

"You heard wrong," I said.

She lifted one corner of her mouth in a freaky half-smile. "We'll see."

"Were you there last night at the festival?" Raven asked.

Milly shook her head. "It was a Friday night. I'm booked solid most weeks. I heard about the murder from a couple who's staying here. Then later Peter called to tell me."

"What about Tara Graham?" I asked.

"What about me?"

We all three whirled around and stared at Tara Graham and Peter Anders standing at the bottom of the stairs. Her arm was entwined through his, and there was a scowl on her face.

I had no idea how to backpedal fast enough.

"We were just wanting to know if Ms. Anders here saw you sneaking around across the street," Raven said. "Since you admitted last night to Brynn that you were walking through her grandma's garden."

Pretty much everyone's mouth dropped open at Raven's boldness.

"Why I never!" Tara said.

"Well, actually you did," I said. "You told me so last night."

Tara narrowed her eyes. "I *meant* I've never been so insulted before."

Doubtful!

Peter scoffed. "Are you insinuating that Tara had something to do with the death of Prudence Livingston?"

I shrugged. "Just covering all the bases."

"I can assure you I had *nothing* to do with Prudence Livingston's death. I can't even *believe* you'd say such a thing."

"So the police haven't spoken to you today?" I asked.

Tara's mouth dropped. "No! And there's no reason they should!"

Did this mean Officer Casen never relayed my concerns about Mayor Barrow or Tara to the chief?

"I won't have you coming over here and slinging mud on someone I care about," Milly said. "Especially since it's obvious it was your grandmother who killed Prudence."

"Thank you, Milly," Tara Graham said, narrowing her eyes at me.

"We need to be going anyway," Peter said. "I have that overnight real estate convention in Santa Rosa. I need to leave within the hour."

Tara flipped her hair behind her shoulder. "And my Seth is going out with his girlfriend later. I better get home and make sure he has something to wear."

Raven laughed. "Does he know he has a girlfriend?"

Tara frowned at Raven. "What does that mean?"

"Tell Seth's girlfriend, the secret to hiding bruises, is to mix an orangish red lipstick in with the toner," I said, pleased I could add something smart to the conversation.

"What are you both blathering on about?" Tara asked.

I grinned. "Nothing."

Let Tara and the girlfriend find out for themselves what a slime Seth was. Raven, Peyton, and I shuffled down the stairs past Peter and Tara.

"Give my best to your grandmother," Tara Graham called out.

The way she said it, so smug and condescending, ripped right through me. I whirled around, and I swear, had Raven and Peyton not each grabbed hold of my arm, I may have decked her.

"Stay off our property," I hissed.

"Be gone," Milly said. "You're not welcome here."

Raven and Peyton dragged me back across the street, practically kicking and screaming. I felt I could rip the Anders siblings and Tara to shreds.

I glanced over at the lighthouse and saw Henley Waller standing at the top of the lighthouse in the gallery, the fenced-in area around the top windows. From his vantage point he could see us, but there was no way he could hear us over the roar of the ocean.

Knowing how he felt about my Grams and Prudence Livingston, I couldn't help but wonder if maybe *he* had something to do with Prudence's death. After all, he'd been at the park last night—the absolute last place I ever thought he'd be. It was just too odd and too coincidental.

"That Tara Graham and her son really piss me off," Raven said as I bent down to unlock the front door.

"I think we need to put one more person on our suspect list," I said.

"Who?" Peyton asked.

"Henley Waller."

CHAPTER 10

"Why him?" Peyton asked. "I thought he liked your Grams."

"I don't know," I said. "Something doesn't sit right with him. I just saw him staring at us as we crossed the street. He has access to our home, he didn't like Prudence, and maybe he saw now as the opportune time to strike."

"But there's no motive for him to do that," Raven said. "Nothing that he gains."

"Revenge," I said. "He gets revenge against both women."

We walked into the kitchen to start lunch, all of us thinking about what I'd just said.

Meow!

I looked down at Jinx. "What're you doing here? We left you at the shop with Grams this morning."

Meooow! Meoww!

I scoffed. "Not my problem she doesn't keep enough food down there. Maybe she's trying to put you on a diet."

"It kinda freaks me out the way you communicate with your cat," Raven said. "And I'm usually down with just about anything."

Peyton laughed. "I've been her best friend since kindergarten, spend just as much time over here as I do my house, and sometimes I *still* think the same thing."

I shrugged and opened a can of Jinx's favorite food. "I don't know how to explain it. We just have this connection."

Meow!

84

I gave Jinx a couple scratches under his chin while he gobbled up his lunch. He purposely ignored me and continued eating.

"Ramen soup for lunch?" I asked.

"Brynn makes the best ramen," Peyton said.

"Sure," Raven said.

I got out green, yellow, and red baby sweet peppers, a jar of jalapeños, bean sprouts, seaweed, mushrooms, scallions, various spices, and a bottle of Sriracha. Peyton diced the peppers while Raven rubbed any dirt off the mushrooms. I grabbed a pot off the hanging pot rack and measured out my water...way more than the package recommended. Once that came to a boil, I added the noodles, spices, peppers, and mushrooms. Setting the timer, I got sodas from the fridge while Peyton and Raven cleaned up the mess.

When the timer dinged, I grabbed bowls and began dishing up the noodle soup for us.

"Now you add the bean sprouts, seaweed, scallions, and whatever else you want. If you like it spicy, put in some jalapeños and a squeeze or two of the Sriracha."

"This is like the craziest thing ever," Raven said. "I can't believe I've never done this before."

"Much better," I said, "than just dumping a package of pre-made spices on some starchy noodles."

We ate our lunch in silence, which I was happy for. I was trying not to overthink everything, but the knot of dread in the pit of my stomach was starting to grow. If something didn't break for Grams soon, they might just arrest her and throw her in jail!

"I'm thinking about calling Aunt Aggie," I said. "Grams is going to be super pissed, but I don't know what else to do."

"Where is she now?" Raven asked.

I shrugged. "I guess still in San Francisco. I messaged her through social media awhile back, and she gave me her phone number. Mostly we just text every once in a while."

"Do you think she'd come help us?" Peyton asked.

"I kinda get the feeling she'd *move* here if she thought Grams could handle it. The last couple texts with her, I think she was feeling me out about it."

"Wow," Peyton said. "Your Grams might have a hard time with that."

Raven snorted. "Maybe Peter Anders can find her a house."

I threw my napkin at her.

"Let's do the dishes," I said, "and then see if maybe we can't find some garden stakes over at the lighthouse."

Five minutes later, the four of us headed outside...Jinx included. The wind had picked up, and I was glad I grabbed my coat.

We sprinted down the street to the lighthouse. I hadn't been inside the place in years. The lighthouse sat on a large peninsula that jutted out into the ocean and steep cliffs gave way to the rocky bottom below.

The ocean this far north was ice cold. We didn't have the kind of beaches where the sand was white or you could drive your car up to the waves. Our beaches had to be hiked to. They were rough and dangerous.

I wrapped my coat tighter around me and followed Peyton and Raven to the back of the lighthouse. Tons of

86

jagged rocks, seagulls, and grassy moss...but no garden stakes.

"What're you kids doin' round here?" Mr. Waller yelled out. We all turned to stare at the red-faced man motioning to us. "Go on! Get away from there! It's dangerous!"

I took point and led the group over to where he stood, still scowling.

"Whaddya want?" he demanded.

I lifted an eyebrow at his surly tone. He was a completely different guy from the one I spoke with last night at the park.

"We want to talk with you about Prudence's death," I said.

He looked down to Grams' house and sighed. "Fine. C'mon in. Get out of this wind."

He held open the metal door to the lighthouse and we stepped inside. The first floor was a museum of sorts. Pictures of the lighthouse over the years, shells, fossils, and other memorabilia circled the bottom half. A spiral staircase sat in the middle of the floor. I leaned over to look up as far as I could and made myself dizzy.

"How many stairs do you have to climb to get to the very top of the lighthouse?" I asked.

"Seventy-six," Mr. Waller said.

Meoooooooowwwww!

"You climb seventy-six stairs every day?" Peyton said. "That's amazing."

"I actually climb more than that if you think about it," Mr. Waller said. "I'm constantly going up and down all day."

"Isn't that—I mean—you know..." I trailed off lamely.

"What? A lot of stairs for an old guy?" he asked.

"I didn't say that," I said.

But I was thinking it.

"Little lady, I've been climbing these stairs for almost forty years. It's what keeps me in shape."

"So you lived here when my Poppa was still alive?" I asked.

Mr. Waller sucked in a breath. "I sure did. Your Poppa and I would sometimes go out together in the early mornings and fish."

"But not the day he died?" I asked.

I don't know why I was asking him so many questions about a man I never met, but with everything that'd happened with Grams, it was like I was afraid everyone I loved was going to be taken from me soon.

"Not the day he died," Mr. Waller said sadly. "Let's go up and have us some tea and we can chat. Will your cat make it up?"

"Yes." I stared down at Jinx. "I'll bring up the rear. Jinx, you stay behind me so we don't trip over you."

Meow!

We slowly made our way up the spiral stairs. They weren't so far apart that it made climbing difficult, but by the time I got to fifty, I was out of breath.

"How on earth do you do this every day?" I asked.

Mr. Waller laughed. "You get used to it."

When we hit sixty steps, I was glad to see a floor above my head. We stepped up into a complete living area. It was mainly a kitchen, living room, and bedroom with another area of the large room sectioned off on the opposite side.

88

"That's my bathroom over there."

I couldn't imagine living in a house where the bathroom was just portioned off. It didn't seem right.

Mr. Waller pointed to another section of stairs that led straight up. "And up those stairs is the lookout and light area. Traditionally called the lantern room."

"This is awesome," Raven said. "I'd *totally* love to live here."

Mr. Waller chuckled. "I feel the same way."

He led us over to a worn Formica countertop and proceeded to get down glasses. "It's a good thing there's only three of you. I have four glasses in this house."

He poured the iced tea and leaned against the countertop staring at us. I didn't know how to broach the subject of either my Poppa or Grams.

"The day your granddaddy didn't come home was the day a little piece of me died," Mr. Waller said. "He and I were childhood friends, you know? Actually, we all three were childhood friends."

"I didn't know." I stared at him thoughtfully. Was that why he always looked so sad standing at the top of the lighthouse overlooking the ocean? He was thinking of my Poppa?

He was nice looking for an older guy...short cropped hair that was more silver than black, hazel eyes, and a weathered face. His shoulders were broad, and he was in good physical shape.

"Was your friendship with my Poppa the reason you asked Grams out all those years ago?" I asked.

Mr. Waller laughed. "There's a lot more to the story of your Poppa, Winnie, and me. But I suppose that's for another time. I'm sure you want to know about Prudence and your grandmother."

"Yes," I said. "I'm really scared."

"I'd always kept my eye on Prudence over the decades. I knew how vindictive she could be. Even after all this time, she still went after Winnie with a vengeance. I tried to tell her it was ridiculous, to let it go, but Prudence was a bitter woman."

"You have to know Grams didn't kill her," I said.

Mr. Waller waved a hand in the air. "Oh, honey, I know that. Your grandma couldn't hurt a fly. She's so kind and soft-hearted."

I almost laughed until I realized he was serious. And while I usually thought of Grams as being kind and generous, I didn't always understand why she was so stubborn and mean when it came to certain things.

"You're probably thinking about her feud with her sister," Mr. Waller said, "but that's more stubborn pride than anything. Winnie was hurt something fierce when your aunt left. It was bad enough half her heart had been ripped out when your grandfather died, but when Aggie left, it ripped out the other half. And then years later when your momma up and left with some stranger, she was left to grieve again."

I wiped a tear from my eye, and Peyton laid her hand over mine. It was brutal hearing someone talk about Grams in pain like that. I didn't want her to hurt. I wanted to make everything better for her.

"And from what I understand," he continued, "you'll be leaving shortly, too."

"I'm not going to feel badly about wanting to live my life," I said hotly.

Meow!

Jinx wound his body in between my legs, like he was trying to give me comfort.

Mr. Waller frowned. "Now, there you go misunderstanding me. I'm not saying you have to feel badly, I'm just saying you'll be leaving and ripping another chunk of her heart away. But that's life. There're always joys and sorrows."

I took a huge gulp of my iced tea, hoping it would push down the lump that was stuck in my throat.

"I wish I could help you girls," Mr. Waller said. "But I didn't see anyone snooping around your place. For all we know, the bad guy may have stolen the garden stakes in the middle of the night and not during the day when you guys were gone."

I sighed. "You're right. I just don't know what to do from here."

"What do you have so far?" Mr. Waller asked.

I told him about seeing Prudence arguing with Mayor Barrow outside City Hall and how he threatened to kill her and the motive behind keeping her quiet due to the new town development plans. He whistled at the thought of the mayor actually killing his mother-in-law. Then I told him about my suspicions regarding Tara Graham. How she admitted she'd come on our property to look at Grams' garden, and how she and Grams have been involved in more than one argument over the remedies Grams sells.

"Imagine a botanist not believing in the healing aid of plants," Mr. Waller scoffed. "It's absolutely ridiculous."

"But I'm not exactly sure the motive behind Tara killing Prudence," I said. "There's really not one, other than to try and place blame on Grams."

"Which would close down her shop," Raven said. "So there is that."

"Yeah," I agreed. "But we didn't find any clues at either house today."

Mr. Waller's mouth dropped open. "You three broke into Mayor Barrow's house *and* Tara Graham's house?"

I waved my hand back and forth. "I wouldn't exactly call it breaking in. We were invited...for the most part."

He laughed. "Oh, you three are something. Reminds me of Winnie and Aggie when they were young."

"Thanks for talking with us, Mr. Waller," I said. "You've shed some light on a few things. Mostly with Grams and my Poppa."

"How's Winnie doing?" he asked.

I gave him a slow smile. "Why don't you come over some night and see for yourself?"

The tips of his ears turned pink. "I just might."

"Don't say anything to Grams," I said, "but I'm also thinking of having Aunt Aggie come for a visit. I know she used to be a bounty hunter, and we may just need her services."

"I definitely don't want to miss that homecoming," Mr. Waller said.

CHAPTER 11

Five minutes later, we were down the stairs and jogging back to Grams' house. It was only two in the afternoon, but it seemed like we'd been at this for days. I was physically exhausted.

"I'm upset Officer Casen didn't tell Chief Baedie about my suspicions of the mayor or Tara Graham," I said as we stepped inside the house.

"Do you want to go to the station and see the chief?" Raven asked. "I'll drive us over there."

"Let's rest for a little bit then go," I said. "I just need a minute to relax and think."

A minute turned into thirty, but soon we had our second wind. Or at least we would once we stopped off at Sisters for some caffeine. Jinx was mad he had to stay behind, but I reminded him he probably wouldn't be welcomed at the police station. I did promise him I'd let him know what the chief said to us. That seemed to mollify him a little as he was ignoring me and methodically grooming himself when we walked out the front door.

Fueled up on caffeine from Sisters, we hit the police station. There didn't seem to be too much going on since we got to park out front. Hopping out from the backseat, I followed Peyton and Raven inside and up to the front desk.

"May I help you?" the woman asked.

"We'd like to see Chief Baedie, please," I said.

The lady looked us up and down. "What's this about?"

"We have some information about Prudence Livingston's murder," Raven said, "and we need to speak to him."

The woman sighed and pushed a button on her desk. "I have three teenaged girls here telling me they need to see you. They have information about Prudence Livingston's murder." She listened for a second then rested the phone on her shoulder. "What're your names?"

"I'm Brynn O'Connell. Winnie's granddaughter."

The woman's eyes widened before she lifted the phone back up to her ear. "It's Winnifred's granddaughter." A few seconds later she replaced the phone. "Take a seat. Chief Baedie be with you shortly."

Shortly was twenty minutes later. He came out from the back, scowled, then motioned for us to follow him. He led us inside an office and sat down behind his desk. He didn't invite us to sit.

"What do you want to tell me?" he asked.

I took a deep breath. "I feel you're missing some vital information with regards to Prudence's death."

"Like what?"

"For starters," I said, "yesterday after school Peyton and I physically saw Mayor Barrow and Prudence arguing about the new town developments going up in Copper Cove. Prudence didn't want the new buildings in town. Mayor Barrow was so mad, he threatened to kill Prudence if she didn't keep her mouth shut."

"Anyone else see or hear this argument?" Chief Baedie asked, not all that impressed.

"I think maybe Peter Anders," I said. "He was walking toward us anyway. If he didn't hear it, he definitely saw it."

"Uh huh. Anything else?"

"Aren't you going to question him?" Raven asked. "That's pretty damning evidence."

"I'll be the judge of that," he said.

I sighed. "Okay. Well, also last night at the park Tara Graham told me she'd been walking through Grams' garden."

He gave me a blank stare. "And?"

"And? Well, *and* that gave her access to Grams' garden stakes, *and* it's a known fact that Tara thinks Grams' shop should be closed down because it's a farce."

"And what's the motive for Tara Graham killing Prudence?" he asked.

I was hoping you wouldn't ask.

"Well, I'm not exactly sure," I admitted. "Maybe to make it look like Grams did it so her shop would close down?"

I knew it sounded more like a question than an absolute answer, but I was still unsure myself.

"What's important here," Raven said, "is that we've provided you with two other suspects."

"Are any of you law enforcement agents?" Chief Baedie asked.

"You know we aren't," I said.

"Well, as luck would have it, I am. I'm actually the chief-of-police in this town, which means what I say goes. And I say none of that is relevant to the murder of Prudence Livingston."

"That's just bullcrap and you know it!" I exclaimed.

96

He stood up slowly behind his desk. "You're gonna want to watch how you speak to me. And I will decide what's *bullcrap* and what's not. And I say nothing you've said changes the fact that Prudence Livingston had a stake plunged into her body with the murder weapon belonging to your grandmother. End of story." He motioned for the door. "Now I need you to leave my office, I have important police work I need to get back to."

"What about Prudence's cell phone?" I asked, grasping at straws.

Chief Baedie sighed. "What about it?"

"Did you find it on scene?" I asked. "Because she had it on her right before she was killed. We all saw her on it, texting someone."

"No cell phone was found," Chief Baedie admitted. "But we have a subpoena in for the phone records. As you can see, we have everything under control here. So you three run along, and stay out of trouble."

We stomped out of the office and followed Chief Baedie back to the front of the station. We hopped in the Mustang and headed back to my house to contemplate our next move.

While Peyton and Raven texted their parents to check in, I messaged Aunt Aggie. I quickly filled her in on what was going on...with a promise she wouldn't say anything to Grams. She messaged me back saying that snooping around the scene of the murder was a good idea, but we needed to be careful.

I was surprised to see Grams and Jinx snuggled up on the couch when we walked in. Usually she didn't close the store on Saturday until five.

"I just couldn't take the constant stream of people," Grams said. "Mostly they stopped in to gawk."

I gave her a hug. "It's not every day someone gets accused of murdering the town troublemaker."

"Ha ha," Grams said.

I waved my hand in front of my face. The sage smudge stick she was burning was heavy and thick in the air. "Grams, I hate to tell you this, but no amount of sage burning is going to clear the negative energy surrounding this case."

"But it can't hurt," Raven said.

I rolled my eyes.

"I'll fix you girls dinner tonight," Grams said. "What're your plans this evening?"

I slid a glance to Peyton and Raven. I didn't want Grams to know what our next move would be. "Just gonna hang out at the festival. It's the last night and all."

Grams nodded. "Sounds like fun. You'll need something hot to stick to your ribs. How about meatloaf and mashed potatoes for dinner then?"

"Yes!" we all exclaimed. Guess all our snooping burned off the ramen we had for lunch.

"You girls go on upstairs, and I'll call you down around five when dinner is ready," Grams said. "I could use some alone time in the kitchen."

We scrambled up the stairs and spent the next hour going over what we'd learned. Mayor Barrow was actively worried that his mother-in-law would derail his plans to expand Copper Cove. Tara Graham had admitted to walking through Grams' gardens around the time the garden stakes had been stolen, and Prudence had a beef with both the

98

mayor and Grams. Also, the number of people in the community who knew Prudence and Grams didn't get along was high, so premeditation for someone to set Grams up would be easy.

"I feel we haven't moved forward at all," I said. "It's still the same thing we knew this morning. Neither suspect had Grams' stakes or bloody clothes hanging around their house. We've really just spun in circles all day."

Raven snorted. "It's obvious the chief isn't going to take anything we say seriously anyway."

"I think we can cross Mr. Waller off the suspect list," Peyton said.

We all agreed.

I bit my lip and weighed my next words carefully. "What if I want to add another suspect?"

Peyton gasped. "Who? The chief?"

I paused at that. Did I want to add Chief Baedie to our list of suspects? What would his motive be? He knew about Prudence and Grams having issues with each other, but unless Prudence had something on him, I couldn't imagine he'd just up and kill her.

"Actually," I said, "I was thinking about Peter Anders."

"Peters Anders?" Peyton asked. "Why?"

"Well, let's break it down," I said. "He probably saw Prudence in front of Grams' store passing out her flyers, plus he's over here at our house at least once a week leaving his business card and pressuring Grams to sell. So he had access to Grams' garden to steal the stakes."

"Okay." Raven wrote down everything I'd said on our list of suspects paper. "And why kill Prudence?"

"Let's say with the expansion of the town development, houses are included in that," I said. "New businesses usually mean more people moving to the area. These people will need a place to live. If Prudence throws a wrench in the plan, Anders could stand to lose potential sales."

Peyton shrugged. "I like it."

"And," I added, "he was at the park last night."

"I think it's good," Raven said. "Should we go check out his place?"

"We know he's gone out of town tonight," I said. "He said he was going to be out of town until tomorrow at a real estate convention. I don't think it can hurt to check out his place."

"You know where he lives?" Raven asked.

I frowned. "Actually, I don't."

"Looking it up now," Peyton said as she scrolled on her phone.

"I think this could be the breakthrough we need," I said.

"As long as we don't get caught," Peyton said. "I don't want to go to jail. It might hurt my chances at college."

"Technically," Raven said, "we wouldn't go to jail. We're still juveniles."

I laughed at the look of horror that crossed Peyton's face. "That's not comforting to Peyton."

Raven grinned. "I can see that."

"I have his address," Peyton said. "Weird. He lives on my street. I never knew that."

"We'll drop by on our way to the park tonight," I said.

A little after five, Grams called us down for dinner. For the next half hour we forgot about the impending problem for Grams and just had a good time. Mostly Raven and Grams talked shop about various plants and their medical benefits. Even Peyton got into the conversation with her limited knowledge. For the first time, I got a true peek at what the three of us girls could accomplish and the direction of our future. I just wish I knew how to apply it to Copper Cove and my struggle to leave or stay.

Once dinner was over and the kitchen was put back in order, I kissed Grams goodbye, promised to stay out of trouble, and to be home by nine. I figured of the two promises, I could guarantee making the curfew.

We hopped in the Mustang and Peyton gave directions to Peter Anders' house. Since we didn't want to be caught, Raven decided to park down a different street, and we'd walk to his house.

"So what's the plan?" Raven asked. "He shouldn't be home, so we can't knock on the door and expect to be let in."

"We knock just to make it look good," I said, "and then we look in windows and see if we can find anything. I mean, if he lives alone, maybe he left the stakes out not worrying someone would see them."

Peter Anders' house was a royal blue, one-story bungalow set back about twenty yards from the street. I went up to the front door while Peyton and Raven headed around the back.

Peeking into the side window, I tried to see if he was really gone. There wasn't anyone moving around that I could see, so I knocked twice on the door. When no one came to the door, I rang the bell, waited, then peeked in the window again.

"Whatcha doin'?"

I whirled around and found Peyton's little brother, Brady, staring at me.

"Nothing," I said, hoping Peyton stayed in the back so she wouldn't be seen. "Shouldn't you be home?"

His small, narrow shoulders lifted. "Mom said dinner wasn't for another half an hour and that I should go outside and play."

"Oh." I waved my hand through the air. "Well, go play."

"Where's Peyton?" Brady asked. "Are you two getting into trouble?"

"No!" I exclaimed. "We're just visiting a friend. Now go away."

His sharp eyes cut to the side of the house, and I groaned when he took off around the corner. Scrambling down the steps, I took off after him. But he was quick for a little kid, and we both rounded the back of the house nearly on top of each other.

"Brynn," Peyton said, "we need to lift Raven up and—" Her voice broke off when she realized her little brother was dancing around next to me. "Brady Alan Patterson, you need to go home right now."

The kid grinned and shrugged his shoulders again. "Okay. I'll just go home and tell Mom and Dad you're breaking into a house."

He turned and started to walk away.

"Grab him!" Raven said.

CHAPTER 12

I reached out and clamped down on his shoulders, pinning his arms to his sides. He tried kicking out, but I backed out of his reach.

"Lemme go!" he hollered. "I'm *really* gonna tell now."

Raven ambled over to where we stood struggling. I could feel Brady getting calmer the closer she got. Okay, maybe not exactly calmer...I think he was about to pee his pants and was numb with fear. And I can't say that I blamed the kid. My first reaction to seeing Raven in her vampire-witch persona had pretty much been the same.

She smiled down at Brady. "I always wanted a brother or sister."

"Why?" Brady asked, "So you could eat them?"

Peyton gasped, but Raven and I laughed.

"Nope," Raven said. "So I could make them do things I didn't want to do."

"What don't you want to do?" he asked, his voice wobbling in fear.

"Be tossed up in the air and look through someone's windows," Raven said casually. "But if you're too scared, I get it. You're just a kid after all."

Brady jerked out of my grasp. "I ain't scared. I can do it."

"Then let's see," Raven said.

Brady shoved past us and marched over to Peyton. "What do I have to do?"

Peyton looked down at her brother then back at us. I gave her a thumbs up.

"First," Peyton said, "you have to swear never ever to tell Mom or Dad what we did here today."

Brady shrugged. "Fine. Now what?"

"I mean it," Peyton said. "You tell and I'll—"

"I ain't gonna tell!" he yelled. "Now, what do I get to do?"

Peyton squatted down and fitted her hands together. "I want you to look around inside and see if you see anything that looks like a skinny spike that could hurt someone."

He scrunched his nose. "Like the Bloodletter in *Fortnite*?"

"Sure," Peyton said. "Something deadly and sharp."

"Cool!" Brady exclaimed. "I can do that."

Peyton lifted her brother in the air, and he shoved his head against the screen and lifted his hands around his head to block out the fading light. Raven and I reached up to steady him.

"Not a lot to see," Brady said. "Just a really messy kitchen. Mom would flip out if she saw this place."

"Do you see those sharp sticks?" Peyton asked.

"Nah. Just some knives in a block like we have next to our stove. But nothing else."

"Let's try the other window in back here," Raven said. "I bet it's a bedroom or something."

We carefully lowered Brady to the ground.

"Ya know, I think we should negotiate my part in this," Brady said. "How about five bucks?"

"How about I let you live?" Peyton said.

"Three bucks?" Brady countered.

Peyton crossed her arms over her chest. "How about I don't tell Mom and Dad about you playing on your X-Box when you should be sleeping."

Brady threw his skinny arms in the air. "C'mon. Give me somethin'! I'm risking my life here!"

"Fine," I said before the two could start arguing again. "We'll give you a dollar."

"A buck?" Brady scoffed. "One lousy dollar? What am I supposed to do with that?"

"Take it or leave it," I said.

He scowled. "Fine. I'll take it. But next time we negotiate *before* I risk my life."

I rolled my eyes as we marched him over to the other window in the back.

"I seriously need to get me a little brother to boss around," Raven said. "I had no idea what I was missing out on."

"She's been doin' it for years," Brady said. "Acts like because she's the oldest she can tell me and Jaylynn what to do."

"That's exactly what being the oldest means," Peyton said. "Now, hush up and get over here."

We lifted Brady back up in the air and waited for his report. "Man, I thought my bedroom was messy. This dude *seriously* needs his mom to come over and help him clean."

"Anything good?" I asked. "Sharp sticks, maybe clothes that look like they have blood on them or anything?"

"*Blood!*" Brady exclaimed. "What did this guy do?"

Peyton gave him a little shake. "Yes or no?"

"I don't know. Hard to say. There are a lot of clothes on the floor and cups and junk on the dresser."

"Having seen how spotless Tara Graham keeps her house," I said, "I'm willing to bet Peter goes over to see her on date nights."

We dropped Brady to the ground, where he promptly stuck out his hand. "Dollar."

Sighing, I dug down into my jeans and pulled out the last of my soap money. "You know this makes you an extortionist, right?"

"If that means someone who gets money to keep his mouth shut," Brady said, "then I guess I'm a 'stortionist."

I slapped the dollar into his hands.

"Pleasure, ladies." He shoved the dollar in his pocket and gave an exaggerated bow. "If you need my help again in the future, I'm available most days."

"Get home," Peyton said. "And don't tell anyone you saw us!"

"I never saw a thing." With a grin, Brady shot out and ran around the side of the house, leaving us to our thoughts.

"I know the killer could have hidden the rest of the stakes," I said, "but I just don't understand. How can we not have found *something* from the three house visits?"

"Let's not get too down," Peyton said. "We still have the murder site to check."

I sighed and followed the girls back to the Mustang. I was trying to be positive, but I was getting more scared as the minutes ticked by and we came up empty-handed.

The park was already packed by the time we found an empty space. I took in a deep breath, and the combination of salty sea air and popcorn calmed my nerves a little. I wanted desperately to believe everything would be solved in the next twenty-four hours, and I could go back to school on Monday no worse for the wear. But I wasn't hopeful.

We'd just passed the games section and were headed toward the cluster of trees where we'd found Prudence, when Seth Graham and his friends stepped in front of us, blocking our path. His nose was swollen and slightly bruised. I was disappointed to see his mom hadn't told him about the makeup tip I'd given her. It really would have worked.

Seth's girlfriend, Mia Larder, crossed her arms over her chest and scowled.

"Well, well," Seth taunted. "Looks like the freak and the nerd have themselves a new friend."

"What are you," Mia taunted Raven, "a witch or something?"

Raven's smile had my heart tripping over itself. She looked downright spooky.

"Something like that," Raven said quietly.

Mia laughed nervously. "You gonna cast a spell on us?"

Raven turned to Seth. "Why don't you share with your friends just how scary I can be?"

Seth's eyes grew wide. "C'mon. We don't have time to waste on these losers."

They were about to turn around and walk away when Raven laid her hand on Seth's arm. "Remember that. Don't *ever* waste your time on us again. You *or* your friends. Understand?"

Seth nodded once, then dragged a protesting Mia and two others off.

"Do you think they'll leave us alone from now on?" I asked.

"They better," Raven said.

Peyton laughed. "No more bullying on our walk home from school? What'll we do?"

"Finally have peace." I turned to Raven. "Thanks. I seem to be saying that quite a bit to you lately."

Raven shrugged then grinned. "Sometimes you just have to know how to talk to people." She jerked her head from side to side, causing her neck to pop. "Or know how to scare them to death."

Peyton and I laughed.

"Now," Raven said, "let's go see what our murder scene tells us."

The three of us linked arms and sauntered over to the cluster of trees. I felt invincible. I felt...loved. I knew Grams and Peyton loved me. They'd been in my life for years. But it had been a long time since I'd felt newly loved...if that made any sense? At that moment, I felt like Raven just strengthened our bond, and that the three of us could accomplish anything.

The crime scene tape was still up and blocked off where we'd found Prudence's body. Which was okay, seeing as how we were looking for hidden items not in the blocked-off zone.

"Peyton, you and Raven spread out over there," I said, pointing to the right of the tape, "and I'll look over in this area."

"Look for anything," Raven said. "Blood splatter, clothing, whatever may help us."

I brought up the flashlight app on my phone and headed to the section of bushes to the left. We were still far enough away from the hordes of people playing and gathered in the middle of the park. It would be a great place to hide something. I didn't expect to find the clothing still lying around, but maybe a fiber or drop of blood to prove it was possible someone else was involved.

I'd just squatted down and shown my light under a bush when a voice stopped me in my tracks.

"What's going on here?" Chief Baedie hollered, loud enough so we could all hear him.

I stood up and slowly walked toward him and Mayor Barrow. Peyton and Raven trotted over, too.

"I told you these girls were up to no good," Mayor Barrow said. "Two of them broke into my home while Lillian and I were at the funeral home."

"Is this true?" Chief Baedie asked.

"I made a delivery of flowers to the mayor's home," Peyton said innocently. "We had an order, and I took care of it for my dad while he was with the Barrows."

"Don't try that nonsense with me," Mayor Barrow growled, lifting his hand and pointing his finger in my face. "I know it was you!"

My mouth dropped open, and I nearly screamed with excitement. There was something brownish red on the sleeve of Mayor Barrow's jacket.

"Chief," I said, "I *knew* we'd find something to clear Grams' name."

Chief Baedie scowled. "What do you mean?"

I pointed to Mayor Barrow's uplifted cuff. "Right there. There's something that looks suspiciously like blood on Mayor Barrow's jacket."

Chief Baedie, Peyton, and Raven all leaned in closer to peer at the mayor's sleeve. He quickly dropped his arm by his side.

"Now, Chief," Mayor Barrow said, "I'm sure it's nothing. Lillian and I stopped off at The Crab Shack to get a bite to eat before coming to the festival. It's probably ketchup or cocktail sauce."

"Or blood," I said.

Chief Baedie stared hard at the mayor. "I'm gonna have to take your coat, Mayor."

Mayor Barrow's mouth dropped, and he started to bluster. "You can't have my jacket! I told you it's nothing. You pursue this, and I'll have your job!"

The chief sighed. "I have no choice, Louis. These kids nowadays, they record everything on their phones. I bet at least one of them just recorded this whole conversation."

Raven lifted her phone in the air. "Right here. I got it all."

"Take that phone away from her," Mayor Barrow said. "She can't record without consent."

Raven laughed. "That's not how it works, Mayor. I know my rights."

Mayor Barrow's face flushed red, and I'm pretty sure I saw a vein pop. "Damn meddling kids! You should know better than to stick your nose into business that doesn't pertain to you!" He shrugged out of his jacket and then shoved it at Chief Baedie.

"This has everything to do with me," I argued. "You're trying to pin a murder on my Grams that she didn't do."

"I'll get this jacket analyzed and cleared up soon," Chief Baedie said. "Don't worry."

Mayor Barrow glared at Chief Baedie then stomped off back toward the festival.

"You kids have done enough damage for one night," Chief Baedie said. "Go home."

Grinning, I motioned for Peyton and Raven, and we took off toward the Mustang. By the time we reached the car, we were laughing and giddy with excitement.

"Well," I said, "we did it! I think maybe this will prove Grams didn't kill Prudence."

"I can't believe it was Mayor Barrow," Peyton said. "And I also can't believe he just got to go free."

"They'll have to confirm it's blood," Raven said. "Specifically Prudence's blood. But it looks good for your Grams."

I hunkered down into the backseat of the Mustang, leaned back, and closed my eyes. "Good. Take me home. I'm exhausted. We'll meet up tomorrow morning at Grams' house to see if anything new developed overnight. But not too early. I'm beat. This sleuthing is hard work."

CHAPTER 13

I heard Peyton's ringtone going off and groaned. I couldn't figure out why she'd be calling me when I told her we'd meet up later. Sighing, I rolled over and snatched up my cell phone.

"What?" I croaked.

"Brynn," Peyton hissed. "Are you awake?"

"I am now." I could feel myself drifting back to sleep and tried to focus on Peyton's voice. "Why're you calling? We said we'd meet up later. Is it morning already?"

"Sort of. It's about one-thirty in the morning."

I sat up in bed. "One-thirty? What're you doing up? What's going on? Are you okay?"

Peyton paused. "It's really bad, Brynn."

"What is? How bad?" My mind was racing. I couldn't imagine why Peyton would be out so late...or so early. "Are you hurt?"

"I'm not, but Tara Graham is."

My heart dropped to my stomach. "Tara Graham? Where are you?"

"I'm at the Graham house," she whispered. "I sneaked outside to make this call. I shouldn't be telling you this, but you're my best friend, and I think you should know what's going on."

"Tell me everything."

Meeeeow!

Jinx entered my room, jumped up on the bed, and started to knead my leg.

112

"Seth came home tonight around midnight and found his mom in the kitchen. She'd been stabbed through the chest with one of Granny Winnie's stakes. He called nine-one-one, and when it was obvious Tara was dead, they called my dad out. He woke me up to tell me. Since I've been going with him on calls, he said the police probably wouldn't question my presence if I wanted to go." Peyton paused, and I could hear sounds in the background. "I needed to move. They're bringing her body out now. Anyway, when I got here, Chief Baedie was questioning Seth. Dad and I went through our normal steps, but I listened more to the chatter of the two other cops here."

"Was the chief mad to see you there?" I asked.

Peyton chuckled. "Oh, yeah. But he didn't argue when my dad reminded him I'd been on every call the last couple months."

"So what are the cops saying?"

Peyton didn't say anything for a moment. "Word is they plan on charging your Grams with this. They think it's cut and dry. Dad said the body hasn't been dead long. Chief Baedie thinks Granny Winnie drove over, killed Tara, and then drove back home."

"That's insane! She's been here all night."

"That's not how it looks," Peyton said. "There was a letter on the table that wasn't here this afternoon when we were here. It looks like it was printed off a computer and says, 'See you at ten.' Then the initial W."

I sucked in a breath. "That's ridiculous."

"I know. Chief Baedie bagged it and gave it to another policeman to take to the station. The policeman just left with the note, and I think—" Peyton broke off, and I thought maybe I'd lost her.

"Peyton? You there?"

"Yeah, sorry. Looks like they called Officer Casen in to help out. He just arrived. I didn't want him to see me on the phone."

"Will they get Grams tonight?" I asked.

"I don't think so. I think the cop that took the note to log as evidence is supposed to sit outside your house once he's finished at the station."

I pinched the bridge of my nose. I was in so far over my head, I didn't know which end was up.

"It's time to call Aunt Aggie," Peyton said. "She needs to get here to help us."

"You're right. I'll call her now."

"Here comes Dad," Peyton said. "I need to go. Real quick, Chief Baedie made it a point to tell me the stain on Mayor Barrow's sleeve was sauce, not blood."

"Crap, that was fast."

"I guess they did a test that showed immediately it wasn't blood. See you at your Grams' around eight. Make sure you call Raven and let her know and have her dad ready, too."

We hung up, and I immediately called Aunt Aggie. I knew Grams was going to rant and rave, but I was tired of taking chances. Aunt Aggie used to hunt bad guys for a living, and we had a bad guy on the loose. We needed her help.

"Hello?" a voice warbled.

"Aunt Aggie?" I asked. "It's me, Brynn. Your great-niece."

Aunt Aggie chuckled. "I know who you are, Brynn. What's going on? Why're you calling so late?"

"It's bad," I said. And quickly filled her in on what had happened.

"I'm leaving now," she said. "I need to pack and close down the house, but I should be there around eight this morning at the latest."

Tears filled my eyes. "Thanks. I know Grams is going to be mad, but I didn't know what else to do."

Aunt Aggie was quiet for a moment. "You let me handle Winnifred O'Connell. This has been long overdue for us."

I hung up and hoped she was right. I didn't want to add more stress to my Grams. I set my phone alarm for seven. I wasn't sure I'd be able to go back to bed, but just in case, I didn't want to oversleep.

I laid back down, gathered Jinx close, and thought about who could have killed Tara. "Do you think Peter Anders is the killer, Jinx?"

Meow!

"I don't know. I guess because it seems awfully convenient for him to have taken a trip out of town. Could he have checked into a hotel in Santa Rosa, then driven all the way back out to Copper Cover just to kill Tara? Timewise he'd have had plenty of time. But why kill her? Other than to place more blame on Grams."

Meooow!

"You're right...it's a stretch. But I'm still keeping him on the table." I scratched under his chin while he purred. "What

115

about Mayor Barrow? Even if it wasn't blood on his jacket, it didn't mean he couldn't have committed the murders. All he had to do was sneak out of his house and go to Tara's house to kill her. Maybe the chief had innocently said something to Barrow and he panicked and this was one more way for Grams to look guilty?"

Meoow! Meow!

I frowned. "You're right. Two things don't mesh. One, whoever killed Tara had to know her son wouldn't be home until late that night. Otherwise why risk going to her house to kill her only to have her son there. And two, what was the mayor's motive to kill Tara? I mean, I could see killing Prudence because she was going to ruin the land development deal for him, but why Tara? Did she maybe find some sort of endangered plant species that made it so they couldn't build on the land site?"

Meooow!

"Of course I know I'm grasping! But it's all I got!"

I must have drifted off to sleep eventually because my phone alarm woke me the next morning, and Jinx was gone from my bed. Sliding my finger over the dismiss button, I sat up to call Raven.

I quickly filled her in on what had happened to Tara, and how the police would probably be at Grams' any minute now to arrest her. She said she'd inform her dad and they'd be right over.

I wasn't even going to mention Aunt Aggie to Grams if I didn't have to. If Aunt Aggie didn't show up until later, then no use having that fight and stress *before* they arrested Grams. I'd deal with that headache tonight. Once we got

116

Grams released, that is. If Aunt Aggie showed up before...well, I wouldn't have to worry about how to tell Grams. She'd figure it out pretty quickly.

Flipping back the covers, I ran to my closet and threw on a pair of jeans and long-sleeved shirt. I ran a brush through my shoulder-length auburn hair, brushed my teeth, and hurried downstairs to make some coffee. I wanted to make sure I was using full brain power when the police arrived.

Grams rolled out of bed around seven-thirty. She and Jinx entered the kitchen, and I quickly filled her in about what had happened over coffee...finishing with she would probably be arrested sometime this morning.

"This is just insane," she said. "I'd never hurt anyone. Who's after me?"

"I don't know, but I think it's either Mayor Barrow or Peter Anders."

I told her the motives behind both men and waited for her input. "It has to be Peter Anders. It's the only thing that makes sense."

"His sister is going to be devastated," I said.

"Unless she's involved, too."

Meow! Meow!

I gasped. "What? You think Milly knows?"

Grams shook her head. "At this point I don't know what I think."

"Winnie?" a voice called out. "You around?"

Grams gasped then scowled at me. "What on Earth is *she* doing here?"

Oops. Looks like Aunt Aggie's here before the big arrest.

A woman about five-feet eight, sixty, slim athletic build, and spiky white hair with neon pink tips stood in the door frame. She had on tight, rhinestone cut jeans with a black bedazzled t-shirt proclaiming *Badass Bounty* Hunter on the front.

I knew I shouldn't be so enamored, but my Grams and Aunt Aggie were complete opposites. Grams was a little older, same body type, studious, and owned her own business. A serious woman who could laugh at herself, but always seemed so proper. Even her hair, always kept long, was pulled back in a tidy bun every day. The woman standing in the doorway was the antithesis of everything Grams stood for.

"Whaddya doing here, Agnes?" Grams asked.

I wanted to run over and throw my arms around the other woman, but I knew Grams needed to process what was going on.

"I heard you might be in a little bit of trouble," Aunt Aggie said casually. "So I thought I'd come see what I can do."

Grams frowned. "You can't do anything. I'm sorry you've come for nothing."

I stood up. "Stop it. Both of you."

I walked over to Aunt Aggie and hugged her. She smelled of lavender soap and leather. An unusual combination, but it worked for her.

"I'm happy to finally meet you," I said. "I've waited nearly eighteen years for this day."

She grinned, a dimple appearing in her nearly wrinkle-free face. "Same here. You got the same hair color as your momma when she was young."

"Seeing as how you ran off when her momma was still young," Grams said, "you wouldn't know—"

"Grams," I pleaded. "I love you, but I need you to put away your hurt right now. Aunt Aggie is here to help us."

"Hmph," Grams snorted. "She's only here for herself."

"Winnifred O'Connell, you know that's not true," Aunt Aggie said. "I'm here for you."

Tears filled Grams' eyes before she could blink them back. "You've only thought of yourself all these years."

Aunt Aggie walked slowly toward Grams. "Right or wrong, I made the decision to leave. I wanted to come back many times, but you never acted like you wanted me here."

"I don't."

I gasped.

"Liar," Aunt Aggie said. "I know you almost as well as I know myself. Even after all these years."

The tears slipped from Grams' eyes, and she quickly brushed them off her cheeks. "You caused me so much heartache in a time I was already hurting."

"I'm sorry," Aunt Aggie said, wiping the tears from her own face. "I just felt like I had to leave. I felt like I was dying here."

I totally understand what you're saying.

"Can we please start again?" Aunt Aggie asked.

Grams rolled her eyes. "Once again you've got crappy timing. Looks like I'm going to the big house for quite a while."

119

Aunt Aggie laughed. "I'm willing to take the chance. Are you?"

Grams did a little more blustering, but I knew she wanted to fling herself at her younger sister. Like Aunt Aggie, I knew Grams about as well as I knew myself.

"Fine!" Grams said. "If I don't go away for twenty years, we can try to make another go of it."

I let out a squeal of excitement as I ran over and embraced the two elderly women. "I *knew* you'd see the light."

Grams kissed my cheek. "Thank you for making this happen."

The doorbell rang and fear gripped my heart and squeezed. I went from euphoria to dread in the blink of an eye. For half a second, I thought maybe Grams should just run. Take off out the back, jump in her car, and drive. She must have seen the look on my face, because she reached over and clasped my hand.

"I love you. I always have," she said. "You're one of the best things that ever happened to me. When your momma dropped you off, I was livid with her. But then I took one look at you and my heart melted. I fell in love right there. You've always been mine."

Meeeooooow!

Tears fell from my eyes. "Please don't answer the door."

"I must." She proudly walked out the kitchen and toward the front door. I quickly followed behind her. "An O'Connell never gives up. Your Poppa taught me that."

120

I grabbed hold of the living room door frame as she swung open the door. I didn't want to drop to my knees in front of the police. I didn't want to show fear.

Aunt Aggie slipped her arms around me, and I held on for dear life.

Grams stepped back and let Chief Baedie and an exhausted-looking Officer Casen in. I dug out my phone and texted Raven and Peyton, demanding to know where they were.

The text hadn't even gone through before two cars came to a screeching halt in front of Grams' house. Peyton, Mr. Patterson, Raven, and Mr. Masters all hurried up the front steps.

"Winnifred O'Connell," Chief Baedie said, "you're under arrest for the murders of Prudence Livingston and Tara Graham. You have the right to remain silent. Anything you say can and will be held against you in a court of law. You—"

Chief Baedie kept talking, but it was like I suddenly went deaf. A hollow ringing in my ears sounded low then grew louder, and black rings appeared around my vision. Jinx threaded between my legs, crying and screeching. Peyton and Raven hugged me, but I couldn't make my body respond.

When I finally snapped out of it, Grams was being shoved into the back of Chief Baedie's patrol car, while Officer Casen got into the driver's seat of his own police vehicle. I looked up and saw Milly and Peter huddled on her front porch. Peter Anders looked like he'd aged ten years.

What's Peter doing here?

I stepped out onto the front porch to get some air...and to get a closer look at Peter.

"Brynn," Mr. Masters said, "I'm going to go to the police station right now. I'll let you guys know what's going on when I get updates."

"Thank you," I whispered.

He got in his car and followed after the police car.

"I'm going up, too," Aunt Aggie said. "They may not let me be with her, but I want to make sure she sees me when they release her."

"You think they'll release her?" I whispered.

"I *know* they will," Aunt Aggie said. "Then we're gonna come back here and figure out who the killer is. I can help you girls."

Her words had me crying again. I sniffed and gave her a hug. "Thanks, Aunt Aggie. I'm glad I called you."

"Me, too."

She jogged over to her truck and sped down the street.

"I didn't think to bring my car over," Raven said. "I just jumped in with dad."

"I'll tell you what," Mr. Patterson said. "Raven, why don't I drop you and Peyton off at your house to get your car, and then you two girls stop by Sisters and get some coffee and breakfast and bring it back here? I think Brynn could use the company."

I nodded mutely.

"We'll be back in about half an hour," Peyton promised as she hugged me.

I smiled weakly and waved them off. Stepping down into the yard, I looked over at the lighthouse and saw Mr.

Waller standing on the lookout, staring after Grams. I then faced the bed and breakfast to see if Milly and Peter were still on the front porch.

They were.

Milly was making apologies to the three different couples who were packing their cars to leave. They waved her off and offered their condolences.

She then whispered something to Peter. He nodded, closed his eyes, and shuffled inside like he was ninety years old.

Once all the cars had left, she glanced over at me. She didn't say anything...just stared. I glared right back. I didn't understand what was going on, but I was sure her brother knew something. He may look like death, but I was pretty sure he was also *responsible* for the deaths.

With one last glare, I turned and ran back inside. Slamming the door closed, I leaned back against it and cried. I wanted to be strong for Grams, but I had no idea what to do. I had no idea how we'd pay for a lawyer, no idea who would keep the shop open if she went to jail. Aunt Aggie had left around the time Grams had opened her apothecary, so I had no idea if she knew the first thing about herbs or sales. Did I skip school to open the shop tomorrow? Was that even legal for me to do?

I'd just plopped down onto the sofa, Jinx rubbing his head against my neck, when a knock came from the front door. I was tempted to tell the person to go away. I knew it wasn't Peyton or Raven...they'd just walk in. Besides, they wouldn't be at the house for another half an hour.

Sighing, I pushed Jinx down and shoved my body off the couch and shuffled over to the door. I peeked through the eyehole and groaned.

Milly Anders.

Meow!

"I have to open the door to her," I said. "She knows I'm here."

CHAPTER 14

I yanked open the door. "What? Can't I have a moment of peace?"

Milly frowned. "It's not my idea to be here, believe me. Peter asked me to come."

"Why?" I snapped, stepping back to let her in.

"He's devastated by what has happened. He wants to know why your grandmother would do such a thing. Also, he wanted me to remind you that if you get into financial trouble, he has a buyer for your house lined up and ready to purchase."

Anger flooded my body. "Your brother is a piece of work. First off, my Grams didn't kill Tara, and it would be a cold day in hell before my Grams would let him sell this house."

Milly shrugged. "I told him I'd ask. I just sent my guests packing a couple hours early. Usually checkout isn't until eleven, but I explained we'd had a family emergency. I haven't had coffee yet. You have any made?"

I had no idea why she was suddenly being so friendly. I could have said no on the coffee, but then she'd know I was lying. You could smell the roasted beans still permeating the air.

"Yeah. C'mon."

I led her to the back of the house and into the kitchen. "How did your brother get here so early? I thought he was in Santa Rosa?"

"Chief Baedie called Peter at his hotel last night around two in the morning. He drove straight to my house."

I reached up and pulled Milly down a mug. I still had my cup sitting on the counter half full. I poured her half a cup. I didn't want her staying that long.

"There's creamer in the refrigerator," I said.

"Black is fine." She blew on the coffee then took a sip. "It's good."

I didn't say anything. This was getting to be too awkward. Where the heck was Peyton and Raven? Where the heck was Jinx for that matter?

Milly took another drink then set the coffee down. "Well, I guess the police will figure this all out in time."

"I guess so."

Milly turned to leave. "It's just too bad your Grams had to go and leave that note on the table. That pretty much proved it was her."

"What?"

Something didn't sound right about that.

"Hmm?" Milly said. "Oh, the note. I heard there was a note on Tara's kitchen table from your grandmother."

I frowned. "How did you hear that?"

Milly stared another second at me before answering. "I think Officer Casen told me. We've been dating for a long time."

I didn't say anything. I tried to recall the phone call from last night. I couldn't put my finger on it, but I knew that wasn't right.

"I'm sure Byron isn't supposed to say anything," Milly went on. "Let's just keep that between us, okay?"

I furrowed my brow. "Officer Casen didn't get to the crime scene until after the note left the premises. At least

126

that's what Peyton told me. Officer Casen didn't get to Tara's house until the body was being led out. The note was long gone."

Milly's eyes hardened. "One of the police officers at the scene told Byron about it."

"When?" I asked.

Milly reached into her cardigan, pulled out a gun, and pointed it at me. "You couldn't just let it go, could you?"

I screamed. "I *knew* you were involved. You've hated my Grams for years. You *and* your slimy brother!"

"Shut up," Milly said. "Stand right there and don't move. I mean it. I'm a pretty good shot. There's no way you can outrun a bullet."

Using her left hand, she reached into her other pocket and lifted out a cell phone. Still keeping an eye and the gun on me, she pushed a button.

"Hey, it's me. We have a problem." She listened for a few seconds then nodded. "Okay. The front door's open."

She clicked off the phone and dropped it back in her pocket. Walking back into the kitchen, she stopped in front of the sink, facing the island.

"So now what?" I asked. "You're gonna kill me? And how exactly is that going to make my Grams guilty? You messed up. Big time!"

A flash of irritation crossed her face. "I have a backup plan."

Jinx slinked into the room, and like a ninja jumped onto the counter and then the refrigerator. Milly never saw him. He sat on his hind legs and watched Milly through narrowed eyes. He reminded me of a black panther tracking his prey.

I heard the front door open and prayed it was Peyton and Raven. I wasn't sure how we could jump Milly without getting shot, but surely with three of us, we could come up with a plan.

But my mouth dropped open when a figure appeared in the doorway. It wasn't Peyton and Raven...or even Peter.

It was Officer Casen.

"What's going on?" he asked.

"Thank goodness!" I cried. "Your girlfriend has gone insane! *She's* the one who killed Prudence and Tara, not my Grams."

But even as the words left my mouth, I knew something still wasn't right. Milly wasn't at the park the night Prudence was murdered. I gasped. Milly wasn't...but Officer Casen was. Or at least he was in the area.

"It's you, isn't it?" I asked. "*You're* the killer. Not Milly."

Officer Casen smirked as he walked toward Milly and wrapped her in his muscular arms. What a pair they made...the fragile bird and the big-strong protector standing on the other side of the kitchen island, wrapped in each other's arms.

"Why?" I asked. "I'm so confused."

"The why is easy," Milly said. "I want this house. Well, I want this house torn down so I can see the view I was promised."

"You're mental," I said. "Totally mental."

"Shut up!" Milly went to leap over the island, but Officer Casen held her back.

"It's okay, Milly," he stroked her hair. "We'll take care of her. We have all the time in the world. Her grandma is just now getting fingerprinted. Think about how miserable her grandmother will be when they find Brynn's body."

That shut me up quick.

"Why? Just tell me that. Surely not all for the house?" I looked at Officer Casen. "And how the heck did you get dragged into this? I've known you almost all my life."

"I fell in love," Officer Casen said as he stared into Milly's eyes. "And when you're in love, Brynn, you'll do anything to make the other person happy."

I made a gagging sound, but they ignored me.

"Isn't he wonderful?" Milly said, standing on her tiptoes to give him a kiss. She dropped back down and nuzzled her head against his chest...the whole time staring at me, smirking.

"We just had to wait for an opportune time," Officer Casen said.

"It's a well-known fact that Prudence Livingston hated your grandmother," Milly said. "She stood in front of her store at least once a week to pass out flyers. That was an easy kill. I also knew from Peter that Tara Graham hated your grandmother. Not only was Tara best friends with Prudence's daughter, Lillian Barrow, but Tara and your grandmother had their own beef with the apothecary." She barked out a laugh. "Seems your grandmother has pissed off more than just me over the years."

There was so much I wanted to scream at Milly, but I didn't know where to start. I caught movement in the doorway. I was pretty sure I saw Raven. Luckily Milly and Officer Casen had their backs to her.

"About a year ago, I met Byron here, and eventually we agreed we just needed to bide our time."

Officer Casen leaned down and kissed Milly on the forehead. "Listening to the love of your life cry about her injustice...well, it nearly broke my heart. I'd do anything for Milly."

"Oh, Byron." Milly patted him on the chest. "You hear that, Brynn? He'd do anything to keep me happy." She rolled her eyes at me.

I looked up at Officer Casen. "So you were at the park Friday night and killed Prudence?"

"Yes. I'd sent her a text from a burner phone. I told her to meet me in that area so I could tell her something about your grandmother. She came eager and excited. I had the stake with me that Milly had stolen out of your grandmother's garden, so all I had to do was stab her."

I thought back to that night. "That's why you were running late to the scene. You'd stabbed her then ran to your patrol car to take off your jacket?"

"I needed to make sure I didn't have blood on me."

"But you told Chief Baedie you'd been on patrol."

Officer Casen chuckled. "Adults lie, kid. That's just a fact of life. After I stabbed Prudence, I went back to my car, took off my jacket, made sure I didn't have any blood on me, and waited to be contacted."

"And with Tara Graham?" I asked.

"Just luck," he said. "Milly knew she was going to be alone since Peter was out of town and her boy was staying

130

out with friends, so around ten Milly texted Tara to see how she was doing. Really to make sure she was alone. Also helps to establish time of death in case the chief wanted to get Tara's phone records."

"And then you just drove over and killed her?"

Officer Casen nodded. "Pretty much. Drove over in an old car I have that no one would recognize, knocked on her door, said I needed to speak to her about her son...and the rest was easy. Milly had typed up the letter, just for added proof against your grandma. Stabbed Tara with the same stake from your grandma's garden. No way Winnifred wasn't getting arrested."

"So now what?" I asked, feeling a little braver now that Peyton and Raven were in the house. "What're you gonna do with me?"

"I'm thinking the cliff," Milly said. "I saw that old man in the lighthouse yelling at the girls yesterday to get away from the edge of the cliff. She's just a kid. No one will be surprised when they find her down below on the rocks. They'll assume she went for a walk to clear her mind since her grandma's been arrested, and she just fell."

I rolled my eyes. "I'm seventeen...not two! No one is going to believe I just happened to get too close to the edge and fell. I've lived here my whole life."

"Grab her!" Milly said. "Let's get this over with."

Officer Casen moved away from Milly...and that's when all heck broke loose.

Jinx dropped down from his high perch onto Officer Casen's head, digging his sharp claws into the policeman's eyes. Officer Casen screamed and brought his hands up trying to fling Jinx off.

But Jinx held on for dear life.

I was about to jump Milly when Raven flew out from the doorway. She ran straight at Milly, did some fancy hand motion thing that knocked the gun out of Milly's hand, and then Raven gave her a flying spin kick that sent Milly sailing backward. It was fast...and it was beautiful.

I ran toward the gun and was about to snatch it up, when Mr. Waller reached down and grabbed it. Peyton casually stood in the doorway grinning, watching as Jinx teared Officer Casen's face to shreds.

Mr. Waller lifted the gun and pointed it at Officer Casen. "Brynn, why don't you try and get your cat off him."

I hesitated. I didn't want Officer Casen to overpower Mr. Waller and take the gun back.

"Don't worry," Mr. Waller said. "This gun ain't goin' nowhere."

"Jinx," I hollered, clapping my hands together. "C'mere."

Jinx immediately stopped pummeling Officer Casen and sprang off his head, landing in my arms.

"You're such a good kitty," I purred. "It's catnip and treats for you."

Meeeoooow!

I laughed. "Yes, for the whole week."

CHAPTER 15

By lunchtime, the whole town was up in arms. Peyton had called nine-one-one to report what had happened, and within minutes, Grams' place was swarming with cops. The good ones. The hardest part was seeing Peter on his sister's porch, dazed and confused.

"I guess I owe you an apology," Chief Baedie said to Grams once everyone had gone. "But in my defense, all evidence pointed to you."

"Maybe next time you'll listen to us a little more," I said.

Baedie narrowed his eyes. "There better not be a next time."

With that, he turned on his heel, stuffed himself behind the wheel of his car, and drove away. Grams wrapped her arms around me and kissed my temple.

"I'm so thankful you girls are okay," she said. "But why ever would you go and do something so crazy?"

"It wasn't crazy," Raven said. "It was the right thing to do. When Peyton and I saw the police car in the driveway, we thought something was wrong. It didn't take long to realize Officer Casen was up to no good."

"And I was watching from the lookout spot," Mr. Waller said. "I saw you get hauled away by Chief Baedie, and then the Anders woman goes over, and then a few minutes later the police car pulled in. Then I saw the girls enter, and I just had a bad feeling. So I figured it was time to put my stubbornness aside and come see if I could help."

A blush spread across Grams' face. "Well, thank you Henley, that was awful nice of you."

133

Mr. Waller also blushed. "You're welcome, Winnie. I always knew you had nothing to do with Prudence's death, much less the Graham woman. We may not have spoken in over thirty years, but a person doesn't change that much."

Aunt Aggie lifted a brow. "Are you telling me you two stubborn cusses haven't gotten together after all these years?"

Grams sniffed and looked down her nose at Aunt Aggie. "Some of us have an image to uphold, little sister."

Aunt Aggie grinned. "Yeah, I see how that image worked for you down at the pokey. You were going on and on about curses and hexes."

"Grams!" I scolded. "You can't go around threatening the police!"

"I can if they deserve it," she countered.

Aunt Aggie threw back her head and laughed...her pink tips dancing in the air. "I've missed you Winnifred."

"What kind of curse were you thinking?" Raven asked. "Because I was gonna go with either explosive diarrhea or male pattern baldness."

Aunt Aggie pointed her finger at Raven. "That's a good one. I haven't done a good explosive diarrhea curse in a long time."

Grams laughed. "Me, either!"

I dropped my head in my hands. "Why me? Why can't I have a normal family with normal friends?"

"Because things wouldn't be near as exciting," Peyton said.

"You got that right," Raven added as she gave Grams a fist bump.

134

***

Two weeks later, Aunt Aggie had her place in San Francisco on the market and was looking for a permanent home in Copper Cove. That's not to say she and Grams were in sync and besties again, far from it. They were both still feeling each other out.

It would take time, but I had faith.

"Did you hear?" Aunt Aggie called a few days later as she barged in through the front door.

"Hear what?" I asked.

Peyton and Raven were sitting at the dinner table. They'd come over to pour over recipes for our Thanksgiving meal we were throwing for our families. We'd offered to cook for everyone at Grams' house.

"I got an offer on my house today...*and* I found the perfect house here in Copper Cove."

I surreptitiously looked at Grams. She knew this day would come, I'm just not sure she was ready for it so soon.

"That's great, Aggie." Grams took a sip of her spiced hot tea. "Where is this perfect house?"

Aunt Aggie grinned. "Right across the street! Milly Anders had to put her bed and breakfast on the market now that she's in the slammer. Her brother agreed to sell it to me at a *steal*...and he's wanting to close quickly. I'm gonna be running the Seaside Bed and Breakfast by Christmas!"

I let out a squeal of excitement and ran to give her a hug.

"And just what the heck do you know about running a bed and breakfast?" Grams asked.

Aunt Aggie shrugged. "Enough. And what I don't know, I'm willing to learn!" She grinned at me. "You ready to have me living across the street?"

In truth...I was. As much as I felt torn between the two women, I couldn't deny that I liked Aunt Aggie. I knew Grams had a long way to go to get over her hurt feelings, but I thought Aunt Aggie was just what I needed. Just what Grams needed. And just what Copper Cove needed.

RECIPES:

Maddy and I have made all these recipes personally, and we absolutely love them all...but especially the scrubs!

Glycerin Soaps

Materials:
1 lb Clear Glycerin (Amazon)
1-2 Drops Soap Colorants (Amazon)
3-4 Drops Essential Oils (whatever scent you want)
*Extra: Herbs: Mint/Sage/*Edible Flowers (Sprouts)
Soap Molds (Hobby Lobby/Amazon)
Knife
2 cup Measuring Glass with spout
Rubbing alcohol
Cling Wrap

Assemble:
1) Cut your glycerin into cubes.
2) Put cubes in glass measuring cup.
3) Microwave 20 second intervals until melted. Do not over melt or you will get foam.
4) Add colorant and scent. If doing different scents, do one soap at a time.
5) If using natural elements like mint or sage, add those herbs to the soap mold.
6) Carefully pour glycerin into the molds, being careful not to pour too quickly. You don't want air bubbles.

7) If you have bubbles, lightly spray or brush the rubbing alcohol over top of soap and they should dissipate.
8) Let sit on counter for about 3 hours. Check. They should be hard enough to pop out and wrap in cling wrap. Store in closet.
9) Should make 8-10 soaps.

*Edible flowers have no pesticides on them.

Sugar Scrub for Hands

*Maddy and I have done a lot of different scents, but Lemongrass/Vanilla, Peppermint, and Orange are our favorites. This is SO easy to do!

Materials:
1/2 Cup Granulated Sugar
2 Tablespoons Liquid Coconut Oil (We used organic)
8-10 Drops Essential Oil (Scent to your preference)
Air-tight glass container (Hobby Lobby)
Large glass or aluminum bowl
Spoon

1) Simply put the first three ingredients in the glass or aluminum bowl and stir, making sure to mix everything well.
2) Store in the air-tight class container.
3) Set hand scrub out in bathrooms or give as gifts!

ABOUT THE AUTHOR

Jenna writes in the genre of cozy/women's literature. Her humorous characters and stories revolve around over-the-top family members, creative murders, and there's always a positive element of the military in her stories. Jenna currently lives in Missouri with her fiancé, step-daughter, Nova Scotia duck tolling retriever dog, Brownie, and her tuxedo-cat, Whiskey. She is a former court reporter turned educator turned full-time writer. She has a Master's degree in Special Education, and an Education Specialist degree in Curriculum and Instruction. She also spent twelve years in full-time ministry.

When she's not writing, Jenna likes to attend beer and wine tastings, go antiquing, visit craft festivals, and spend time with her family and friends. Check out her website at http://www.jennastjames.com/. Don't forget to sign up for the newsletter so you can keep up with the latest releases! You can also friend request her on Facebook at jennastjamesauthor/ or catch her on Instagram at authorjennastjames.

Made in United States
Orlando, FL
26 April 2023